# Thurso

## P. James Callaghan

Published by Armley Press 2019
ISBN: 978-1-9160165-0-7

# Acknowledgements

Copy editing: John Lake
Cover design: Mick Lake
Layout: Ian Dobson
Production: Mick McCann

Thanks to Gareth Durasow, Lucy Jackson, Hamish
Ironside and Sally-Ann Dale

*For my wife*

# SUNDAY

## 1

Perhaps he'd be safe in Thurso.

David Prudhoe had surfaced about ten minutes ago. Now, he stood in a lay-by staring at the passing traffic, relapsing into half-trance states then coming round to reality. He scurried off, aware of his vulnerability. He was too exposed out in the open. He had to keep moving. It would be all over if he kept still. He hurried towards the village, working his way over uneven, filth-sprayed grass between the road and the grimy crash barrier. Weekend lorries loomed up behind him; some gave short horn blasts. He didn't hear, or listen.

How had he come to be here? He remembered the lorry driver: over-friendly, glad of the company. The cab was warm and smelt of milky coffee and sweat. He knew he had to keep moving and this seemed to be the most logical way of doing it. Speedy, direct.

The driver's cheery, one-sided conversation had welled up like crude oil in a clear sea. And David had surfaced with it.

"Further north the better, that's what I say," the driver said and David moaned. Moaned. "You all right?" David felt him throwing glances at him across the cab. "Not travel sick, are you?"

David shook his head. He wasn't travel sick. He'd surfaced from the depths he'd been drowning in for the last few hours (days? years?) and he knew now that being in this lorry, on a road, with people, was now dangerous.

The driver continued with his chatter. If he asked David questions, he didn't answer. David flicked his eyes around his new world. He had to go north – he knew that already – and he had to keep moving. If he didn't keep moving he'd die.

How did he come to be in this lorry? He remembered gliding across the gentle rise of the Black Isle – the early sun glowing through a low ceiling of creamy cloud. He remembered walking out of Inverness, north, towards Kessock Bridge. The lorry had stopped. They climbed up the southern slope of the Isle, away from the town. The fields and woods rolled by, silent and hypnotic, and the babble of the driver's talk covered him like a warm blanket.

But now it was different. Something had made

him rise up. What it was didn't really matter.

He flew over Cromarty Firth, the pale light yellowing. And he knew he had to get out, to escape from this human noise and smell, to forget all trace of it.

"Can you drop us off here, pal?" he murmured. (Had he interrupted the driver?)

"You what?" A pause and then: "Here?"

"Yeah. Please."

"Well, I'll wait till we're over the bridge, shall I?" The driver sounded English. (Yorkshire? Manchester?) He had a large red face with a dense moustache. His eyes were little gashes. He swung the wheel and the lorry lurched onto the lay-by next to a snack bar with its shutters closed.

"Looks like breakfast'll have to wait," the driver boomed, nodding at the snack bar. David was looking at him sidelong, squeezing himself against the door. He heard the driver's music playing (Boston? Chicago?) and the lorry came to a stop. David pulled the door handle.

"Thanks," he muttered and jumped out.

"No problem, sir." Like a mock sergeant major. "Good luck."

David had slammed the door shut and walked towards the back of the lorry as it hissed and chugged and then roared away.

Now he was standing at the side of the road, staring at traffic. He took his back pack off and unzipped it. There were a few apples and a plastic bottle full of off-pink liquid. He vaguely remembered packing them. Now he'd need other things if he was to go north across country. He would have to stay away from the roads, be ready for all weathers; he'd need food and shelter. He shouldered the pack and stared at the languid Sunday traffic again. He didn't know for how long. The day was brighter. A car horn slapped him and he scurried off.

Now he was walking towards Evanton, beneath a dark green hill. He realised he had the light-headed, floaty feeling of a night without sleep. He followed the sign to the left, off the main road. A short train clattered across a bridge over the road and he watched it disappear through sparse trees. He took a bend in the road to the right and saw the low, stone buildings of the village. A few pubs, a grocer's shop, a post office and two outdoors shops. He tried the first one but it was dark inside and the door was locked. He looked at the sign and it said it opened at ten. He patted his left trouser pocket for his phone but it wasn't there. So what? It was before ten. He backed away from the shop and looked along the street. An old couple was walking their dog on the other side of the road. He pulled his hat tight down and moved off, staring at the pavement.

The other outdoors shop was across the road, where the old couple had just walked. He let them pass before crossing over. The lights were on and he pushed the door open. A little bell tinkled above his head. The shop was empty and smelled of new tents. He hesitated, holding the door open. Somewhere, wistful folk music was playing. He walked forwards and immediately saw something he needed. As he examined it, a petite, young redhead appeared and took her position behind the counter.

"Morning!" she sang. David took a half glance at her, ignored her. She was wearing a black tee shirt with a band that he'd never heard of, a dark green long sleeved tee shirt underneath. Black combats. "Can I help you?"

David glided round the shop, grabbing things he needed. When his arms were full he off-loaded on the counter. He flicked another glance at the girl. Freckles and pig tails. She was looking down, trying to put some of the stuff on the counter in order, so he quickly went back before she got a look at him.

It only took another armful to get what he needed and he dumped it on the counter. There was dried food on a rack next to the counter and he snatched random packs. He could hear the pips of the till, and then the girl spoke again.

"We've got a special offer on Kendal Mint Cake. Three for two today, if you're interested." A beautiful, lilting voice – almost in harmony with the music. He grabbed three packs off the pile to acknowledge what she said. Best that she didn't hear his voice. Don't make eye contact either. The girl was packing his things into large, glossy carrier bags. He put his hand in the thigh pocket of his walking trousers and pulled out a roll of twenties and tens. He was half surprised to find this. A vague memory came back to him.

If the girl had noticed the money roll she didn't comment, but he quickly turned his back and pulled out a few twenties. The shop was warm and he was wearing his thermals as well as a fleece and waterproofs. He could feel sweat behind his knees, and his scalp prickled and itched. He stuffed the roll back into his coat pocket as he heard the girl announce the total cost. Turning round, he heard her say something else, something about the weather. Such a beautiful voice. He stared at the bags on the counter as he handed over the money.

"You'll be well kitted out anyway, wherever you're headed." The heat was rising; he felt soaked. He grabbed the carriers and launched himself back towards the door. "Do you not want your change?" he heard her sing, but he didn't want his change if it meant hearing that voice one second more.

He gulped the cool air outside and continued up the street. Except for safe, far-off figures it was deserted. He found a bench in a little flower garden that was set back off the street next to a pub. He sat down and thought of the plan as he unpacked his new kit and arranged it for ease of carrying. The plan was all that mattered now. The means and the end. There could be no distractions, no hurdles. It was simple. He would follow rivers, not roads. He'd seek the shelter of woods, not the lights and harsh lines of houses and inns. He had to keep moving and he had to go north. To Thurso. He'd be safe in Thurso.

## 2

The boy sat cross-legged at the edge of the cliff. He felt the cool grass tickling his calf and his hand shot down to give it a quick, efficient scratch. His other hand spun a buttercup round by its stalk. He heard a seagull cry somewhere above and craned his head trying to find it. Squinting and gurning, he scanned the sky but gave up. He'd seen seagulls before.

He continued to gaze out across the sea to the islands. The Old Man of Hoy stood watching, grey and stalwart under a bright sky. The sun was high above and a few feathery cirrus clouds hovered above the horizon to the east. He'd learnt about cirrus clouds at school. They did a project about the weather. Miss Palmer had talked about clouds one afternoon and Ali had been transfixed. By the names mostly: stratocumulus, nimbostratus, lenticular. "Lenticular," he mouthed. He'd miss Miss Palmer. Brilliant white cumulonimbus clouds, like colossal Buddhas, were piling up beneath the horizon. He wondered what it was like to be underneath one of those clouds.

Ali liked to sit at the top of the cliffs before he made his way down to his den. He usually had something to watch: a container ship maybe, creeping east to west, from Norway to Canada, he'd guess. He'd follow it until it became invisible.

"New flower," he said, throwing the old, wilted one away. He picked another one, the largest he could find, and began spinning it between his thumb and forefinger.

"How far?" he said and thought about the first land he'd come across if he sailed directly north. "Iceland? The North Pole?" Was there land at the North Pole? He'd probably find out when he started at high school.

He picked his nose with his free hand. He managed to tease a nice, dry bogey out but it had a moist thread that stretched and then snapped back onto his upper lip.

"Pesh," he spat. He threw the buttercup away and mopped the snot with the back of his hand, then wiped it on his Spider-Man tee shirt. He would've wiped it on his trousers but Dad had made him wear shorts again. The dry bogey next. He started rolling it and settled back down into staring at the sea. A light breeze occasionally whispered in his ear. Another over-head seagull. The muffled, industrial clatter of the docks to his right, down below.

He thought that maybe he was putting off building his den. He hadn't thought it through properly when he came up with the idea. He needed a place to go, a secret place that not even Dad knew about. But the more he worked on it, the more he thought it was a bad idea. It was quite a treacherous climb down to the cave and it was cold and damp and noisy. Getting his tools and materials down there hadn't been easy either. It was difficult to sneak anything out of the house, let alone big stuff like wood and shovels, without Dad noticing. And he had to take the tools back to the house each time so that Dad wouldn't miss them.

"Alistair," Dad had said this morning. "Have you taken the last apple again? What have I said about telling me when you're about to take the last apple? How will I know to buy more apples if I don't know you've taken the last one?" They were all questions that Ali wasn't supposed to answer.

"Sorry, Father."

"Okay. Now go to your room, think about what

you've done."

He would have to finish the den. He had the rest of the summer to do it. He wanted it to be somewhere he could sleep, somewhere he could live if it came to it. If he ran away, this is how he would do it: first from the house, then from Thurso.

## 3

David left the village behind for the pine forest and the hills to the north. Pylons marched away along the flank of the hill and he followed them for a while until he started to feel exposed. He disappeared into the trees. Wide tracks criss-crossed the forest and he followed one around the shoulder of the hill, following the pylons.

He took his coat off and slung it over his shoulder. It was becoming muggy, even though a fine drizzle was filtering through the branches above.

The track fell down the hillside towards a quiet road so he followed a rough path that took him into the trees. He walked parallel to the road down below, staying away, staying high. Above his crackling footsteps and his breathing, he could hear distant voices: shouting and laughing behind the curtain of trees ahead. He slowed his walk then paused for a moment. The path rose up to the top of a rocky hillock. The shouts were getting closer. He looked off to the sides and thought about hiding when a man on a mountain bike flew over the brow in front. David dived out of the way of a flash of lime green and looked back to see the mountain biker glancing back.

"You okay, buddy?" the biker called then disappeared into a dip. The shouting seemed to be at either side of the path now, weaving through the trees. He sprang to his feet and clambered up the hillock away from the path and any other track. His heart pounded in his ears and sweat leaked into his eyes.

He climbed to the top of a hill and into an empty clearing. He knew now that he had to stay hidden. He couldn't afford to get that close to anyone again, or it would be Game Over. He hunched his way across the clearing, darting looks like a bird; he was soon back under the cover of the pines. He tried to stay to the contours of the hill without getting too close to the road. He paused and took his brass compass out of his hip pocket. He flipped the lid with his thumb and held it up. He looked around and moved off to the northwest. The plan was to make for Loch Morie and then follow the southern shore up the glen to higher ground.

Now the forest gave way to open moorland. Again he stopped and looked at his map. It was in a transparent plastic pouch that dangled from his neck. He must've bought it at the shop earlier. "No other way." He'd have to cross this open ground, using the cover of the woods and plantations that hugged the hillsides. "Like swimming in shark-infested waters. Between islands."

The day was trying to brighten and he lifted his face towards the warmth that filtered through the branches. He found himself humming – almost whispering – to himself as he walked. He scanned the land as far as his neck would twist, a practice that would develop into a habit over the coming days. He was alone on his little circle of earth. The first wood he came to sloped down to a track that forded a trickling burn. He decided to follow the track, welcoming the more even ground, but soon it started to descend to the valley. It was here that he looked over towards the loch and saw cars parked up. The reds, yellows and whites were out of place. He stared for a while and the hillside crawled with blue and purple dots. They seemed to be climbing up from the valley. There were hundreds of them. He crouched down and nibbled the dried skin around his thumb nail, staring with blank, black eyes. Those little dots made him feel sick.

The southern tip of the loch lay around the shoulder of the next hill. By the time he got down there the little dots would be all around him. He looked over his shoulder at the forest he'd just left. He liked that view better. Again he looked at his map. "That's me here." He fingered the map. "Strath Rusdale." Forest all the way up the glen. "Until the road runs out." He let his map pouch hang and felt in his thigh pocket for the Kendal Mint Cake. He looked again at the dots and turned away, back into the trees.

## 4

Fraser could remember his wife's face. He just chose not to, if he could help it. He still talked to her though, in his lonelier moments. He wasn't mad or anything.

He just liked to chat to her now and again, to keep her abreast of current events, to report on the boy. "Don't know where he's got to." He glanced up at the crucifix he'd bought from a gift shop at Carfin Grotto. "Made his favourite for him. Cheddar cheese and pickle. So ungrateful. All the things I do for him. Doesn't even come home for his lunch."

The cheese sandwich was gone and his cigarette ash threatened to drop onto the crumb-speckled plate. The sun shining through the Big Room window was making the side of his face hot but he wasn't going to draw the curtain. The Big Room was his favourite place in the house. His Big Chair was in the Big Room. And the television, his books. There were still the relics from the days the boy's mother was still around: her pathetic attempts at painting, the coffee table she'd made out of an old pallet and her mother's wall clock, which he'd stopped winding years ago. He would've thrown all these things on the fire but he didn't have anything to put in their place.

He sipped at a tumbler of warm lager. Frank Sinatra sang somewhere, unseen. "Three Coins in a Fountain". Muted and flat as in a waiting room.

"I'll be having my Sunday treat tonight," he told the crucifix. "What should I have? Black bean sauce. Chicken or prawn? Or chilli beef? Chinese, anyway. None of that Thai shite that Gary brought up that time." The ash dropped onto the plate. "And a wee dram or two, of course." He topped his glass up. "I'll be having words with the wee bastard when he finally gets in."

## 5

It was overcast again. David threw an apple core into the long grass of the haugh he was striding across. He scanned the surrounding trees for movement. He may as well have been walking through savannah. "Scanning for lions."

A footbridge led him into the pines again and up and around a conical hill. He smiled and hummed as he rose above the floor of the glen. The track ran high above the river and the road beyond. Level, peaceful fields lay either side of the river, which wriggled black and torpid between isolated cottages. He could hear the distant buzz of wood being sawn. Soon the road down below disappeared and the valley split as he came across a burn running down from the west. He crossed it in one long stride to keep his boots dry and clambered over a dry-stone wall. Ever northward. He followed the contours of the land, keeping a distance from the river, which now rambled in his right ear. He climbed a small hillock; the forest opened into brown moorland where he rested, taking a couple of mouthfuls of squash. He would soon be at the head of the valley. He looked back and saw only trees. "Good." Onwards, and he started to hum again, striding across small gurgling streams. At the valley head a small loch lay black and still. The wind played on the surface. He took his map pouch and pack off and lowered them to the ground where the water lapped the rocks and earth. He tucked his coat underneath, feeling the breeze cooling his wet back. Then he was on his belly, cupping a hand into the water. It tasted funny and he spat it out.

He knew Thurso was northeast but that Lairg was also. "On the plus side, it's mainly through forest." But could he chance going through a whole town? The thought filled him with profound dread. "Stay away from towns. Stay away from towns."

He realised how quiet it was and he held his breath to emphasise it. All he could hear was lapping water and the blood pumping in his ears.

A voice said: "That'll do you no good."

He blinked and looked at the water.

Another voice said: "They'll get you, sure enough."

David moaned. "Not you."

"You evil cunt. You think I'd leave you? Uh? All alone? You're evil, son. You need telling."

"Shut up."

"I haven't even started yet, son."

"Shut up." He covered his eyes with a grimy hand.

"Evil wee bastard."

"No."

"You're a sinner, my boy. A sinner. And the sooner we get you in the water, the sooner we'll wash all that sin away."

"Shut up. Please." But he was already thigh deep in the loch.

"Get yourself in, son. Wash away those sins."

"He needs to be fully submerged."

He lost his footing on the rocky bottom and fell backwards, twisting on himself. He threw his hands up as if trying to find something to hold on to. The water badunked and white foam swirled and sloshed as his head plunged under the surface. But then he was up on his feet, lumbering and moaning like the living dead towards the shore. He dropped to his knees and then his hands, spitting water. Willing a towel to be in his pack, he slipped his hand to the bottom, felt the dry soft flannel there.

As he scrubbed his hair he heard a skylark or some other bird trilling high above. Then, again, silence.

## 6

Ali breathed in the smell of Chinese food as he tried to close the front door so it didn't make a sound. It was no use.

"Alistair? Come in here." Dad's paper-and-comb voice floated through the house. He never had to shout; he barely raised his voice. Ali thought about climbing the stairs but that would make things ten times worse. He felt the heat of the house on his cheeks as he prised his trainers off and padded into the Big Room. Dad was sat erect in his chair, his hands cupping his knees. A cigarette smouldered in the ashtray he'd made at school, next to his Sunday night whisky.

"It's late. Where've you been to?"

"Out."

"See, that's the kind of thing we were talking about the other day." Ali watched the black inside of Dad's mouth. "You've to give a proper answer when I ask you a question, agreed?"

"Aye."

"Aye, what?"

"Aye, Father."

Dad's lips stretched into a tight smirk. His eyes were like stab wounds. "Come over here. Standing in the middle of the room like a lamp. So again. Where have you been?"

Ali noticed a purple scab among the sandy stubble of Dad's head. He remembered when he was younger and his hair was like Demerara sugar candy floss. His face was redder than normal. He must have been drinking all day. "Near the loch." Dad didn't like him playing by the cliffs.

"Who with?"

"No one." Ali tapped the edge of the table with his fingertips. He looked at the picture of Dunnet Head that Mum had painted. It was hung behind Dad's chair. He would often have to look at it.

"And what's the rule about when to come home?"

"Before it gets dark, Father." Tap tap tap.

"Before it gets dark, Father. It's more than fair, this time of year. Agreed?"

"Aye, Father."

"Stop tapping, boy. You're like a fucking metronome."

"Sorry, Father."

Dad scratched his forearm, freckles tightly packed. "Your dinner's in the bin. You'll have to go hungry. And you missed your lunch too."

"Sorry, Father."

"Aye, well, pour me another dram, then you can go. Agreed?"

Ali picked up the bottle. He had to hold it with both hands to stop it shaking. "Good lad. Who's the Boss?"

"You are, Father."

"I'm what?"

"You're the Boss."

"Good lad. Off you go." Ali placed the bottle back on the table. It was nearly empty. He stepped back, turned and made for the hallway. "Alistair." He stopped and turned back. "You know I love you, don't you?"

"Aye, Father."

"Good. Good. You're all I've got." He took a sip and leaned back. "Thank fuck you've got your mother's hair."

"Can I go to bed now, Father?"

"Aye, son. Off you go." Ali walked towards the stairs, his heart pounding. "Get yourself a glass of milk. But drink it in the kitchen." Ali faltered. Maybe that offer was a trick. He eased the Big Room door shut and climbed the stairs. Maybe the den was pointless. A lot of effort for nothing. He would have to run away from Thurso as soon as possible.

But then Dad would be all alone.

## 7

David thumbed little circles on the lid of his compass. He rubbed his head and dropped another few branches on the fire, which cracked and smoked in the clearing he'd found. He was surprised and glad to find the flint in his pack. There were other things in there too, some of which he'd brought from home and the others he'd bought in the village. A fishing line, hooks, a few pans, a good knife. He wished he had a torch.

He must've taken up the girl's offer of cheap Kendal Mint Cake: there were six bars in his pack. His main concern was food. He'd never had a large appetite but he'd be walking over seventy miles over the coming days and the Kendal Mint Cake wouldn't be enough. He rooted about in the bottom of his pack and brought out a few packs of savoury rice.

"Nice. Nice rice. Rice is nice."

And the apples. He would have to ration them. One per day.

"Fish it is, then."

He sat back against one of the trees his tarp was tied to and tilted the map towards the fire.

"Evanton", he saw the village was called. He traced the path he'd taken with a grubby finger. "Strath Rusdale". Now he was in Amat Forest, remote and roadless. "But not deserted." The thin sounds of the night, when people went to their homes, surrounded him like a wet towel. At times his head would jerk at a sound that wasn't quite right.

The night kept the air damp and he worried about whether his clothes would be dried by morning.

"At least I kept my coat dry, eh?"

He looked up at patchy clouds playing around the smirking moon. He wouldn't sleep much tonight. He wouldn't be happy until he was in Thurso.

"Thurso. Get to Thurso."

But he wasn't sure why. He was born in Thurso

and he'd spent happy holidays there after they moved to Aberdeen, when he saw more of his dad. During the summer holidays they'd spend a week with his Auntie Liz, Mum's sister, before catching the ferry to Stromness and then to Rousay, where his dad's favourite camp site was.

The fire was dimming. An unexpected breeze made the embers glow and fizz. The trees leaned in on him. The nearest one said: "You think you'll be safe in Thurso, my boy."

"Aye." Then he stiffened. "Fuck off."

"He's got another think coming about getting to Thurso in one piece."

"You said it. They'll track him down, gut him like the pig he is."

"Dirty sinner."

"Shut up."

"Fucking dirty pig sinner."

"Fuck off."

"You'll never get to Thurso."

The air grew still again, as if dying.

## 8

Rob was dreaming. It was the same dream. The one he used to have when he was a boy. A dream without images: only a feeling of overwhelming dread, like something terrible was about to happen or something terrible had just happened and he was still feeling the aftermath. And the sound. Someone above him was pounding a sledgehammer into the floor.

He always awoke after a few seconds, the memory of the relentless pounding a ghost in his ears, synchronised with his pulse. The feeling of dread always persisted for a few minutes. In the early days he would wake her and she'd wrap her arms around him and whisper to him until his eyes narrowed and his heart slowed. She'd stopped having to do this after they were married; he'd not had the dream again in all that time. Until now. This time he knew he wouldn't wake her up. If he turned over and brushed against her she usually shrank away.

He went back to the old method of calming himself: thinking of something good, something he loved. When he was young it was ice cream. He didn't know why; he'd never liked it particularly. It must've been the first thing he could think of, the first time, and he'd not found any reason to change it. He smiled at the memory as his breathing slowed.

He lay on his side, on the edge of the bed, facing away from her. She was almost a mirror image of him and there was a gap between them that a child could fit in. Now he was wide awake in the brown darkness. He propped himself up on one elbow and listened to her purring and the babble of the pump in next door's pond. His jacket and jeans hung from the coat hook on the back of the bedroom door and made the profile of an enormous face.

She was sat at the base of the statue of George Stephenson outside the Engineering Department at university when he first saw her. She was wearing a tattered, black leather jacket over a dark green shirt and a purple top. Maroon tights and a short, frayed, denim skirt. She sat hunched over a book with her feet at twenty to four. Her black Doc Martens were painted with faded little flowers. At her feet a large canvas bag was slumped against her calf and she rested her free hand on it like she was preventing a cat from running off. Her hair was her natural tarnished-brass colour. It was quite messy and she had to keep tucking it behind her ear as the wind took it.

Rob was amazed he had taken all this in. He remembered staring at the curve of her thigh and hoping for her knees to part ever so slightly. That curve was the sexiest, most beautiful thing he'd ever seen.

She looked up from her book and glanced around. He knew at this point he should look away but he couldn't. Then she caught him. It was just a glance but then she looked back when she noticed him. He kept staring at her and then she broke away and her eyes defocussed and flicked to some point to his right. Then she must have remembered her book and she looked down and pretended to carry on reading. Rob remembered the trace of a smile.

Now they were in the house they bought together in the bed they bought together. She was as far away from him as possible without sleeping on the floor. He wanted to roll over there and put his hand on the curve of her waist, nuzzle her ear. But he knew he wouldn't.

In the morning he would drive down the street where they lived, turn right onto the main road and leave her behind.

# MONDAY

## 1

Rob sat in the passenger seat of his car working on a large egg sandwich he'd bought from a village shop a few miles back. It wasn't a bad sandwich. The bread was fresh and there was plenty of filling. Maybe a little too much mayonnaise, making it sloppy.

The lay-by was empty except for an estate car from Holland. There was a large, blue sign saying "Welcome to Scotland" and, underneath, "Failte gu Alba". Beyond, the green and yellow hills tumbled away into a pale haze. Radio 4 murmured under the buffeting wind.

It had been easy enough to sneak out of the house without waking her. During the night she'd moved into the spare room. She'd been doing that more and more lately. He'd wake up, sensing her absence, even before he slid his arm across the mattress like he was trying to find a lost ring.

He'd got dressed – boot cut jeans, green tee shirt – and taken his wallet and car keys, and eased the front door shut. The early morning was fresh and cool under a cloudless sky, scarred with lonely contrails. He drove north past pine copses like sleeping beasts and hillsides peppered with sheep. He passed two or three cafés and pubs that claimed to be the First and Last, and he stopped in one for breakfast.

There was a young blonde behind the counter and he ordered a black coffee. She turned to the machine and checked the hopper. "I need some more beans. Sit down if you want. It won't be long."

"It better be wide, then." The girl humoured him with a tight-lipped smile. "Eh?" he added. Maybe she didn't get the joke.

He sat at the nearest table and read the papers. The blonde brought his coffee over. "Where are you from?" she said.

"Yorkshire, tha knows. Born and bred."

"You must've set off early."

"No. I live in Ponteland now. Just outside Newcastle." The blonde nodded. "Just out for a drive." Rob glanced at her purple lipstick. She gave the same smile, half rolled her eyes and walked off.

He sipped his coffee as it became tepid; he wasn't in any rush. Gail would wake up soon and text him.

He wondered why he'd brought his phone. Maybe something from his subconscious had told him to, or maybe it was just habit.

Later, he drove through a tree tunnel, sunlight strobing through the car, where the scent of freshly cut grass seeped through the air vents. He remembered lying on his back in the park all those years ago with her head on his shoulder and her hand stroking his chest. Her falling asleep and his trying not to move for fear of waking her.

The road had risen and wound up a barren valley towards the border, the land undulating all around, dotted with isolated, strange and ancient hills. Alone, ever moving, smiling: an elation of freedom had swollen in his chest.

Now, he finished his sandwich, wiped his mouth with his hand and got out for a stroll. The land dropped off beyond the opposite lay-by. An oil tanker had just pulled away and now he stared at the last of the Pennines beyond a neat dry-stone wall: soft, forever hills blanketed here and there with dark pines.

His phone buzzed in his pocket. He took it out and tapped IGNORE then turned it off. He'd send her a text later, to reassure her. He didn't want her to worry.

**2**

It was getting light. Cool air licked his temples and ears. The sky was orange and red and purple. The trees were starting to wake up. The birds were gathering. David drank from his water bottle and stared across the valley to the south. He gave his head a brisk rub. It felt greasy and itchy.

He'd slept in a little hollow halfway up the steep, wooded hillside. He left the camp as he'd found it, scattering the cold ashes of the fire and scraping earth and pine needles over the spot with his boot. He scanned his map then packed it along with his sleeping bag and tarp.

He zigzagged up the hillside through the trees and soon he was at the top of the ridge. The sun shone vermillion between the land and a thick layer of low cloud. It would be a tough walk this morning. He would be heading north, crossing valleys rather than following streams and rivers. He could turn east and follow the water but there were too many houses and roads. The other route would be worth it. He inhaled; there was an earthy, woody smell, like beetroot or pencil shavings. He set off down into the valley. The map had said Strath Cuileannach. "Strath Cuileannach." He rolled the syllables around his mouth like ice cubes.

He created his own path through freshly cast gossamer and he spat air and brushed his nose and beard as he walked. At times the sun hid behind cloud and the world became muted and sad. He rushed onwards in search of the light.

At the foot of the ridge he found a footbridge over a tree-lined river. He looked around and saw a farmhouse further downstream. The path from the bridge took him past an old barn, which he eyed as he skulked past. Then he was crossing the end of a single track road that seemed to go past the farmhouse. He could hear people-sounds that way and stared towards them as he melted into the trees.

There was no path here and he started climbing again. The map showed another plantation on the hillside but the land was scarred and brown. He could hear heavy machinery and wood being sawn and he scanned the valley looking for its source. He followed a burn to the top of a wide pass, a saddle of land between two craggy peaks. Looking back and down the valley, he could see a huge machine cutting down trees. It was a monster with one massive arm that swung around. David saw it grab the base of a tree trunk and cut through it in seconds. It stripped the bark from one end to the other and then cut the trunk into logs. He stared for a while as the machine-monster worked its way along the hillside, eating the forest. Then he realised there must be a man in the machine so he scuttled off.

Ever northward. He dropped into the next valley, where the pines were still growing. Most of his water was gone and his thighs and knees were throbbing. He found a burn and filled his bottle. This time the water was clear and sweet. He followed the burn out of the plantation and onto rough heath. Soon the land flattened and then rose again. David felt like he was on a boat on the sea. At the top of the next ridge the forest was thick, lusher, more natural. It fell down the wide hillside and many converging streams cut through it. David continued north, away from the water. He bounded across trickling streams and felt his thighs going wobbly as he tried to control his descent. His path emerged onto a narrow road and he stopped short. There were sparse houses up and down and he backed into the forest. The land across the road was open and green. He studied the tree line beyond and thought there might be water there. A dark patch caught his eye – darker than the other greens surrounding it. It may have been a shadow or it may have been a dark cloaked figure, not moving, just staring. David wasn't sure if the figure was watching him but he took a step back, dropped to his haunches and sobbed silently into his fist.

## 3

He couldn't find the boy. Fraser stood with his hand on the newel cap, stroking the polished globe like a fortune teller. "Alistair?" Silence but for the hiss of the rain against the landing window. The boy had gone upstairs after breakfast. He must've sneaked out of the kitchen when he was washing up. "Alistair." Why was the boy this way? He blamed his mother. Just like her. "If I have to come up there." He'd had to climb the stairs on previous occasions when he'd been ignored, something he avoided doing if he could; his knee ached sometimes when it rained. He'd had to redress the boy for his disrespect. He'd said he'd not heard him calling out his name. Calling out his name for five minutes until his head hurt. That was another trait from his mother: dishonesty.

Fraser decided to go upstairs; it was nearly shower time anyway. He worked his way up, feeling the warmth of the thick carpet between his toes. Why was

the boy so insubordinate when he tried his best –
under the circumstances – to raise him right? He
pulled himself up with the banister. His knee throbbed
in protest. The tenth stair creaked and he wondered
how the boy had managed to miss it on his way down.
He rested on the landing and felt the weak sun
filtering through the stained glass. He leaned against
the banister.

"Alistair!"

Again, silence.

## 4

Three boys, each about fifteen and full of the energy
and group bravado of that age, were shouting,
laughing and pushing each other outside Gail's house,
a mock-Tudor semi with black timbers and clay fish-
scale tiles above the bay windows.

The street was otherwise quiet and litter-free, the
kerbs bordered by lush grass verges and the
pavements edged with low, red-brick walls with
small, metal signs saying STRICTLY NO PARKING.
Some of the gardens had signs saying PONTELAND
RESIDENTS SAY NO TO WIND TURBINES.

Gail didn't mind people parking their cars outside
the house: not many people had a need to; but she did
mind kids hanging around there. She remembered
what she'd been like at that age but she felt no
empathy for the teenagers. They were harmless
enough – just three friends from further down the
street from fairly nice families – but they were

annoying her. Their tinny, good-spirited shouting resonated through the double glazing and Gail heard herself tut as she glared at them through the kitchen blinds.

She liked her kitchen; they'd had it extended recently. The prevailing colour was white: large floor tiles matched perfectly with the high-gloss doors and drawers. In contrast, the work tops were black faux granite. She'd wanted real granite but Rob had said they couldn't afford it.

The boys were sitting on the garden wall now. There was a fine drizzle; the front garden was one of the few in the street to have a tree near the road and they huddled underneath it. She liked having the tree – an old sycamore. Gail had wanted a house in Darras Hall up the road when they moved out of their flat in Newcastle. It was leafier and there weren't as many kids.

She thought of Tom at work.

Normally she'd roll the blinds up and knuckle the window a couple or three times but she didn't feel like it today. Her stomach felt tight and her palms were moist. She wiped one on her dungarees while she looked down at the screen on her phone. She sniffed once – wet and noisy – but even now she enjoyed the warm smell from her elevenses coffee.

She'd been phoning him all morning. Each time it went to voice mail she'd texted and when he hadn't replied she'd sent another one, and another. Only now had he replied. The text said he'd gone to Phil's for a few days. That was all. No explanation. No apology. Tears welled again and she dabbed her pink, swollen eyes with her sleeve. She thought of Kielder Water, of the last time they'd gone there a couple of summers ago and Rob had fallen in trying to get a branch. She didn't smile at the memory. They were going there for the day today; they'd both got the day off especially. A special day. Their anniversary.

She twisted the blind closed and walked away from the window. She took another look at her phone, thinking he might have replied to her last text and maybe that her alerts tone wasn't working. Nothing. She sucked in a big sob then screamed and threw the phone across the kitchen.

## 5

David took his pack off; the map showed a bridge over the river past a group of cottages. He became clammy at the image. Upstream there was a footbridge. He walked west, keeping to the trees as long as he could, glancing at the buildings to his right. There didn't seem to be any movement there. The country opened up and he strode across boggy scrub, alert and furtive, like a deer. From a broad hillock he could see the footbridge beyond a series of dry-stone walls.

The grass felt spongy underfoot. He climbed the first wall and heard harsh voices behind. He twisted round. Running towards him across the field were a dozen or more police, shouting and waving short heavy sticks. He jumped from the wall and pain shot up the side of his ankle and he let out a mournful yelp.

He lost his balance, tried to right himself and landed in a twisted pile on top of his pack. He forced himself to his feet, moaning, then peered over the wall. The police were almost upon him. David hobbled across the field towards the next wall, twisting to see the police clambering over the last.

From somewhere uncertain, he could hear a strange, liquid music; the air tasted acrid, metallic. If he could only remember what he'd done wrong.

He vaulted over the next wall, taking care to land on his good foot. Again he saw the police swarming across the field behind him. He could see their faces, contorted with rage, vengeance. There were more of them than before. He dashed for the last wall across a smaller field. He didn't look back. A road flanked the river beyond the footbridge. It was deserted and he skipped across and disappeared into the thick pines. The strange music faded out. He found a thick trunk and crouched down behind it, looking and listening for his pursuers. A single car passed and the white noise of the engine gave way to the white noise of the river. His panting subsided.

He would have to stay as far away from the roads as he could from now on. He climbed away from the river and the road. He left the trees behind and trudged across bleak heath. The top of the ridge was spattered with small lochs and he cringed at the memory of the Man telling him to jump in. He stopped for water and crouched, staring into the distance. The land sloped gently down to the east, carrying plantations above the River Cassley. His head twisted back and forth like a CCTV camera. He rubbed his head to get rid of the spiders and continued north. The new rain was cool on his face.

### 6

Ali watched the buses come and go. Thurso bus station was really just a fancied-up bus shelter near the train station. His bum kept going numb on the narrow plastic seat. He stood and walked around. The rain crackled on the plastic roof but now he was almost dry after the walk from the house.

He'd been careful when leaving. He'd packed his raincoat in his backpack so it didn't rustle and he'd held on to the handrail as he missed out the tenth step. He'd heard Dad singing along to the Rat Pack as he washed up and he'd pressed the door handle down as he eased it shut after him.

He'd missed the last one but the next bus to Inverness would be here in thirty-seven minutes. From there he'd get the bus to Aberdeen. At Aberdeen he'd look in the phone book for Auntie Fiona's number and she'd pick him up from the bus station and she'd take him back to her house and he'd live with her.

Auntie Fiona was Mum's sister. The last time he'd seen Auntie Fiona was just before Mum died. He didn't know what happened with Mum. Whenever he asked Dad, he'd tell him to stop asking stupid questions. Ali had not gone to her funeral: he remembered Dad going out in the morning in his suit and Dad's mate Stu and his wife Liz being in the house with him. It was raining and it felt like a

Sunday but it might have been Friday. Stu was very quiet and Liz would leave the room now and then with tears in her eyes. Ali played with his Lego next to the fire. Dad came back when it was dark. He was drunk. Stu and Liz had slept in the guest room next to Ali's.

Auntie Fiona would have to take him in. He would make her swear not to phone Dad and have him pick him up. He'd have a new life in Aberdeen. Sure, he'd miss his pals. Well, Ewan, anyway. And Miss Palmer. They wouldn't miss him though: they'd forget about him soon enough.

## 7

Rob drove through another tree tunnel, the lowering sunlight flickering through the pines to his left. The scent of the trees filled the car and he thought of Gail: the last time they'd shared a shower. Then he shook the memory from his head.

He was following the River Tweed in a steady line of traffic. He had Prince's eponymous album on and contributed sporadic humming to "I Feel for You". The original was far better than Chaka Khan's cover.

He'd driven through red-stone Hawick to Selkirk, where the road wound down the hill through the town, onwards to Walkerburn and Innerleithen, following weaving, wooded roads along the river up the valley towards Peebles.

He glanced to his right and saw an elderly, sun-tanned couple pushing mountain bikes along the road. They had matching pure-white hair and maroon raincoats. Something about them made him feel that they were very happy together. They'd been cycling since they got married decades before and had travelled every road in Scotland. He allowed himself a smile.

Nearing Peebles, the road slowed and he passed a stone bus shelter where two teenagers sat kissing. They looked like one person. He wound the window down. "Go on, lad!" he shouted and laughed. "Eh?" The teenagers stared at him. He drove on, cackling. The traffic in front slowed to a halt. The road was straight and flat and he could see some kind of blockage further ahead. "Shit," he hissed. "Ah, well." He turned the volume up to listen to "Sexy Dancer".

It looked like the oncoming traffic had stopped too. Maybe he was going to be here for a while. He turned the engine off and Prince stopped playing. He wound the other window down and heard unseen birds chuntering above the low rumble of idling engines. The air was heavy and still. He could smell the heady fumes of their exhausts.

After a few minutes a policeman in a high-visibility jacket came walking up the middle of the road. He was stopping at every car and speaking to the driver. Rob leaned out as he approached his car. "Afternoon, ocifer," he chimed.

"Afternoon, sir," he replied in his soft Border accent. "There's been a serious road traffic collision ahead. Both sides of the road are blocked so we're advising drivers to either wait until the road's cleared or you can turn back."

"How long?"

"I couldn't tell you at this time, sir."

"I'm going to Glasgow. Is there…?"

The officer started to walk off. "You can either wait until the road's cleared or turn back, sir."

"Okay, cheers," Rob called as he walked off, and under his breath: "He enjoys his job." He sat staring at the car in front, wondering what to do. Phil was expecting him at seven. There was no telling how long he'd be stuck here but he wasn't sure where the detour would take him. He changed the CD. 1999. What would Gail be doing about now? Probably having a cry. Throwing some stuff. She didn't like being ignored. He stifled a pang of guilt. The text he'd sent her would suffice. It was a pity about today. He liked Kielder Water.

Or maybe she was with Tom from work. He wasn't really friends with him; more of a friendly colleague. He said hello to him most mornings. When Tom started at the office a couple of years ago Gail had clicked with him straight away. Maybe something to do with his being tall, black and athletic. He and Gail would go out with the rest of them for drinks after work on Friday, something Rob didn't like to do much. He saw those people all week; he didn't want to develop the relationship any more than he had to. She and Tom had become quite friendly over the years. Close even. They were clearly fucking.

The driver behind was revving his engine. He probably had been for a while. Rob looked in the rear view mirror and saw a couple of young idiots who were mainly teeth and spots. The driver had an aggressively stupid expression. Rob opened his door and walked towards the car. The lads saw him coming but the engine kept revving. Rob stood at arm's length from the driver's window.

"The fuck are you doing?" The lad stared at him for a moment then relaxed his foot. The engine idled again. "Maybe turn your engine off?" he suggested and backed away towards his own car. "We're going to be here for a while."

Back in his car he opened the glove box and unravelled the wire from around the sat nav. He plugged it in and started to programme it. "Turn around when possible," it said. Her name was Diane and she spoke with a generic Home Counties accent.

"I haven't told you where to go yet! Stupid bitch." He found Phil's postcode in his phone contacts and entered it.

"Turn around when possible," Diane said.

He stared at the screen. "I'm not going that way." He tossed the sat nav onto the seat and listened to the birds wittering. A breeze whispering through the trees was drowned by the idiot behind starting his engine. He turned round and reversed his car opposite Rob's and shouted "Wanker!" before screeching off.

"Your dad's arsehole!" Rob replied. He smiled and shook his head. "Youth is wasted on the young. The cunts. George Bernard Shaw."

He thought about turning around himself and finding a diversion but he wasn't in any rush. It was getting late and he was tired so he thought he may as well stay at Peebles for the night. He picked his phone up off the passenger seat and switched it on. There were umpteen missed calls from Gail and a few texts.

He phoned Phil but it went to voice mail.

"Yeah, Phil, you big bugger. It's Rob. I'm going to be a day late, it turns out. I've been held up at, er… Peebles? I think it is. Some inconsiderate bastards decided to crash into each other and they've blocked the road. So I'm going to stay here tonight. I'll be there tomorrow. You'll be working tomorrow, I assume, so I'll potter about Glasgow until about, er, sevenish? See you then. Bye." He tapped the little, red phone icon and thought about phoning Gail. The phone started playing the *Get Carter* theme and the screen said "Gooey calling". He turned the phone off and threw it onto the passenger seat.

They lived together but she'd left him years ago. Soon after they were married, actually. Maybe she thought the same about him. Who could tell? Women were bonkers. Well, all the women he knew.

What if he just left the car and walked into the woods?

## 8

She felt a little flutter in her midriff as she slammed the taxi door and walked towards the Maharaja Spice restaurant, avoiding a puddle that had established itself in the uneven pavement. She glanced up at a crescent moon peering through a ring of flitting silver clouds.

The restaurant was unassuming, sandwiched between a post office and a closed-down carpet shop. Gail had been once before but barely remembered the details. They'd been for Alice's birthday last year; she lived in Gosforth too, like Tom. She remembered breaking her rule about drinking too much wine but she had a vague recollection of everyone having enjoyed the food. Tom swore by it. He said he'd had everything on the menu.

The place was warm and dimly lit, with deep carpets and paintings depicting Hindu deities. Tom sat studying the menu on a dark leather chaise longue opposite the bar, a half of lager on the low table in front of him. A waiter floated over to her and she gestured towards Tom. "I'm meeting my friend." The waiter cocked his head, smiled and retreated to the bar. Tom saw her coming and smiled his big white smile. He got up and kissed her cheek – a combination Rob had never done – and they both sat down.

"It's busy tonight. For a Monday," she said.

"Always is in here."

The waiter came over with a menu. "Like a drink?"

"Please." Tom answered for her. "Pint of cider?"

"Mmm, yes, please," she said to the waiter, who cocked his head again and floated away.

Gail blew out and rolled her eyes. "What a day." She took her lipstick out of her bag and noticed Tom's scowl. "Anything wrong?"

"With me? No." That deep, rich voice. "You seem to be in much higher spirits than earlier. When I spoke to you."

She was just barely controlling herself so she didn't start crying. "How was work?" She unscrewed the cap and gave her lips a once over.

"Same old same old. Tony's back. He seemed to have had a good time. Red as a lobster, though."

She sucked her lips in then pouted. "Lucy fancies Tony, you know."

"Really? I thought they were just good friends. Like us."

She looked at him, held his gaze for a moment then put her lipstick back in her bag. The waiter brought her drink and she took a large gulp. She spilled some as she put the glass down, noticed the red smudge on the rim. Somewhere Indian music was playing. "This saxophone sounds like 'The Final Countdown'. The keyboardy bit."

Tom listened. "Yeah," he laughed.

"Have you decided what you're having?" She picked up the menu.

"I will have...the lamb pathia." She scanned the menu and felt Tom staring at her. "The prawn madras is excellent in here," he said.

She looked for it. "Where is it?" Tom leaned in and their shoulders touched. He felt firm and hot. Tom pointed to the seafood section and backed away. "Oh, it's got cinnamon in."

"I thought you liked cinnamon."

"I do. Cinnamon is just... sex. Except in savoury stuff. Can't get my head round that." She looked at him and he was gazing at her as if she'd just laid bare her soul. She blinked and glanced over his shoulder. There was a man stood at the bar with a shaved head. He was standing with a petite woman in a black dress. "Don't look now," she murmured, half-covering her mouth, "but there's a bloke at five o'clock whose head is almost a perfect sphere."

Tom blurted out a laugh. "I'm not even going to check that's right."

"No, you've got to. It's like a football with ears." She started scanning her menu again. Tom laughed again; it was like a thick, warm duvet. He looked slowly over his shoulder with a nonchalant expression. Gail looked down at the taut muscle on the side of his neck then down at his chest. He turned his head slowly back to her and she looked up to meet his eyes. His broad shoulders rocked as he sat hunched over in silent laughter then let out another belly laugh.

"I'm right, aren't I?" Gail giggled.

The waiter came over with a tray. "Your table's ready." Gail went to pick up her drink. "Yes, please," he said and put the pint and half on the tray.

They walked through a subdued babble to their table in the back corner. The waiter pulled out Gail's chair and lit the tea light. "Are you ready to order?"

Tom looked at Gail. "Have you…?"

"Can I – just give me few more minutes?"

"No problem," the waiter said and disappeared.

She scanned the menu again, not really reading it. "What shall I have, Tom? Tom, what shall I have?"

"Do you want chicken? Or lamb or fish?"

"I fancy fish."

"Fish masala. No cinnamon."

She found it on the menu and said: "Sounds good to me. Fish masala it is."

She slapped the menu shut and picked up her pint. They clinked glasses and took a sip each. "You didn't manage to get in touch with him, then?"

Gail felt herself flush. "No."

"He's an inconsiderate bastard."

She cringed at his candour. "He just goes sometimes. He just needs to get away, to get his head sorted."

"What does he need to sort? Why can't he talk to you about it? Whatever's bothering him."

"He's always been like that." She could feel her eyes flickering, like broken butterflies. "That's just him. I just let him get on with it." She took another swig, leaving less than half the pint. "I'm just pissed off he didn't tell me sooner. I've wasted a day's holiday today."

"How long's he going to be gone?"

"I don't know. He won't answer his phone. I'm not making excuses for him but he's quite – sensitive really. He makes out he's confident and charming, which he is, but I know him and it's all a front most of the time."

"Maybe I could have a word with him. When he gets back."

"I don't think that'd be wise. I think he finds you... not intimidating but –"

"Intimidating? Why?"

"Because you're fit." She made a point of laughing. "In a sporty way. Athletic." She cleared her throat and her eyes flickered again. "He just needs to get away sometimes."

She looked across the room at a good-looking couple. They were maybe in their fifties but they looked after themselves. The woman was sun-tanned and well-dressed. From what she could see of him, the man was handsome with a matching tan. He too wore expensive-looking clothes. Their faces glowed in the light from their phones. She was hoping that the man would pass his phone to the woman to show her something amusing but they just both sat in the cosy dusk of the restaurant, swiping their screens.

Gail felt a pang of self-pity but shook it off.

"What are you thinking?" Tom muttered.

"Mmm?"

"You floated off then."

She took another drink. "I was thinking I could do with another pint."

## 9

The sun was lowering towards High Ormlie when PC Gary's car slid to a stop in front of Ali's bench. He wasn't really a PC. He was a sergeant but when he was younger he and Dad were police constables and that was what Dad said Ali should call him. The rain had stopped but the air was still damp. Pink and violet altocumulus clouds hung over the sea.

"Young Alistair." PC Gary wasn't in his uniform. It must've been his day off. He looked at Ali with the look of subdued surprise that he nearly always had, even when he wasn't surprised.

"Hiya."

"What are you up to?" PC Gary said with a look of feigned suspicion. Ali looked down and started scuffing his heel against the pavement. "Does your dad know where you are?"

Ali lied. PC Gary stared at him, nodding, his wrist resting on the top of his steering wheel. A gust of wind blew a circle of litter around just outside the shelter.

"You'll be wanting to go home for your tea, no?"

"Aye."

"What are you doing? Sat here in the bus station?"

"Just resting. Having a rest."

"You been playing with your pal. Ewan, is it?"

"No. He's on holiday."

"Right." PC Gary leaned over and opened the passenger door. "Get in, then. I'll give you a lift home." Ali pulled the handle of the back door and climbed in. PC Gary looked over his shoulder. "Suit yourself," and pulled the front door shut. The car was clean and tidy and smelled nice. "Belt up in the back, young sir." Ali did as he was told. He pressed a button and the window slid down. "Home, James," PC Gary called out and the car eased away from the kerb.

They drove down Traill Street in silence. Ali watched the last of the shoppers and office workers rushing across the zebra crossing before the car swung onto Olrig Street. As they passed the police station, PC Gary said: "So where's he gone to, Ewan?"

"I don't know. Cyprus, I think."

"Cyprus. Very nice. How's your dad, anyway? I haven't seen him for ages."

"You came up last Christmas."

"Aye, that's right, I did. Looking after you all right, is he?" PC Gary smiled. "Or are you looking after him?"

Ali didn't answer. He didn't know how.

## 10

Phil Collins was all right when Peter Gabriel was in Genesis, when he just played the drums. But then Peter Gabriel left and Collins started singing. Then when he went solo… The low volume of the music seemed to make it even more awful in the soft murmur of the bar. The hotel was to Rob's liking: the Georgian façade with its bright green woodwork; bare, stone walls inside; flags of St Andrew's cross and the Royal Standard hanging from the high beams; pastel green panelling; comfy, brown leather armchairs. But Phil Collins was starting to irritate him. Almost as if two songs with clashing, dissonant keys were playing at the same time. It was "One More Night" so he was hoping that the CD was a compilation of 80s power ballads.

He looked around the bar for distractions. Middle-aged men sat alone at high tables clutching pints of lager, taking the afternoon off to read the paper or watch the football, which played silently on a large screen above the bar. A young couple at a table for two leaned into each other. Rob saw more of the woman than the man, who whispered in the woman's ear. She leaned back slightly with a look of feigned shock but then smiled and, looking sidelong at her boyfriend, blew a kiss from the corner of her mouth. Rob felt lonely for the first time since leaving Gail.

A well-dressed woman sat with her knees together

on a Winchester sofa reading a book he wasn't familiar with. Her hand, which belied her youthful looks, enveloped a large cup. She smiled to herself now and then without any self-consciousness. Rob was willing to overlook her age; the woman was a cracker. Her blackened eyebrows were like curly brackets that had neatly fallen over and her full lips twitched sometimes as she mouthed the words that she read. She crossed her legs, exposing the long curve of her thigh. Rob was glad to see that she had no wedding ring, as if that made a difference. One side of her white bob was tucked behind her ear. A lock escaped but she left it hanging. Rob felt himself getting hard. He smiled at himself and looked away then drained his pint.

He went to his room and had a wank in the shower, thinking of the woman. He thought of her there in the bath, stood up, bent over, the edge of the shower curtain in her tight fists as Rob fucked her from behind. If he saw her later he'd make a move on her.

## 11

Fraser yanked the door open. His scowl turned to a cautious smile. "Gary."

"Fraser," Gary sang. "How's it going?"

Fraser glanced down at the boy, opened the door wide. "Very well. Very well. Where did you find this wee tumshie?"

"I found him loitering with intent in the bus

station."

"Was he now?" Fraser was still smiling. "What kind of intent, I wonder." The boy glanced up as he edged round him. Was that a look of defiance on the wee cunt's face? Almost a smirk. He looked sidelong at the boy, over his shoulder. "Get yourself a drink. Your supper's in the oven." He looked at Gary and rolled his eyes. "As usual. Thanks for bringing him back, Gary."

"No bother."

"Thought you'd be away for the summer."

"No. Well, we had a week away in June but we thought we'd just have one of them staycations."

"A what?"

"Staycation. It's when you're on holiday but you stay at home."

"Right, right. Well you've picked a good week for it. Except – " Fraser scanned the sky above Gary's head. Rain clouds were starting to gather again.

"Aye. It's been better, weather-wise. Back in at the weekend. Nights."

"Right. How's the Inspector? Still – "

"Basil? Aye, he's still there. Being... Basil Fawlty. Doesn't give me as much lip, though, these days."

"Aye, that's right. Sergeant Maitland now, is it not?"

"Aye, but you can keep calling me Gary if you want."

Fraser copied Gary's laugh. The first few spots of rain started to fall. Gary looked up and stepped forward. Fraser took a step back against the door and planted his palm on the opposite wall. Gary looked at him funny then smiled.

"I'd ask you in, pal. I've got stuff on at the moment."

Gary gave him another funny look. Still judging him after all these years. "Aye, well, that's fair enough, Fraser."

They nodded during the silence, then Fraser said: "Anyway, I'd better – "

"Aye, don't let me keep you." Gary turned towards his car. The rain was getting heavier now. "Hey, Fraser. You know where I am if you need me."

"That's very kind of you, pal." He watched Gary start his engine then backed into the house, waving. His face felt numb from smiling. Then he closed the door and went into the kitchen. The boy was sitting at the table, swinging his legs and stuffing leftover fried rice into his mouth.

"Who's the Boss?" The boy stopped chewing and stared. "What have I said about making me repeat myself?"

"You're the Boss, Father."

"Can you not remember the wee chat we had last night?"

The boy was silent. He still had a mouthful of rice. "Aye, Father."

"Swallow your food, leave the rest and go to bed." The boy chewed once and swallowed. "I'll deal with you tomorrow, you insolent cunt." Fraser watched the boy as he pushed away from the table, the chair feet honking on the tiled floor. He didn't enjoy disciplining the boy; he found no pleasure in it. But the Lord – in his wisdom – had given him the task of raising him alone and he was going to do it right. The boy scraped the plate and rinsed it at the sink. His wee, slender arms and legs. Pale, translucent, like ivory. The boy turned. His blue eyes almost violet. Like his mother's.

He would discipline the boy tomorrow. He was tired now and he'd need his strength.

## 12

Rob dried himself then lay naked on the bed that was too soft, listening to the noise from outside. Some people were having an argument but they were too far away to tell what it was about. The room was stuffy and he couldn't get used to the pungent smell of lavender. He felt himself nodding off so he rubbed his face and stood and caught himself in the mirror by the door.

Recently he was noticing new places where he was gaining weight. His biceps had lost their definition a while ago; now his body had decided that his belly was big enough and it was going to divert fat to his groin. His cock seemed to be shrinking by the week. He lifted his gut and turned side on to the mirror. He let it drop and slapped it. He blew out, deflated.

He dressed and went down to the restaurant for an early dinner. The restaurant was empty but for the couple from the bar, cupping each other's hands across their table. They looked up at him as he swayed in. They looked disappointed at having their privacy broken.

Rob ordered a pint of the stuff he'd had when he arrived – a heather ale from a local microbrewery – and the venison casserole. The beer was citrus and floral, the sauce was heavy and rich and the meat tender and strong, but he left most of the carrots. He had a double whisky for afters. A twelve-year-old single malt. As he was sipping the last of it, the woman from the bar walked in. She floated with small, shy steps, holding her book to her full, round breasts. She sat away from the others, placing the book carefully on the table. Rob sat over the whisky, twisting his wedding ring round his finger.

He realised for the first time that she looked like an older version of a girlfriend he had at university. Before he and Gail got together. Sarah, she was called. He'd shagged her a couple of times and he remembered the time he brought her off when she was in the bath. But then he'd gone out one Thursday and got drunk and had literally bumped into the girl he'd gawped at near the statue of George Stephenson outside the Engineering Department. The girl with flowers on her boots.

Rob finished the last four sips of whisky in one draught and went upstairs to bed.

He dreamed that someone was taking a sledgehammer to the floor upstairs again. He awoke, gasping, and slid his hand to the other side of the bed, searching for Gail. He felt like he was the only person on earth. When he thought of her his breathing slowed. She was his ice cream now: her firm lips, her pale skin, her green eyes, her musical laugh, the messy, red bob of hair, the curve of her hips. He felt his pounding heart relax. He swung his arm over to the bedside table and picked up his phone. There were no more missed calls or voice mails. He brought up Gail's name, stared at the screen for a moment then let it fall onto the mattress.

## 13

He dreamt of Sheldon.

They were friends once, before everything changed. They went to school in Aberdeen. David couldn't remember ever being happy at school. He often looked back on that time, cringing, cursing himself for the stupid things he'd done, some worse than the things he'd do later in life. Almost.

Sheldon was a bit of a nutter. When he was bored, he used to lie down in the middle of the street. He wouldn't move when cars came. Just to piss them off. David and the others would sit on the edge of the kerb laughing until it hurt. That was one of the good times. Another time, they were walking home from school. Sheldon took his leftover sandwiches out of his bag and kicked them around the street, aiming at cars and shop windows. If they didn't stick, he split them apart and smeared butter over the windscreens.

That was before. When they got a bit older they drifted apart. They found new friends and greeted each other in the corridors between lessons with curt hellos.

It was during this time that Anne-Marie came along. She seemed to appear from nowhere, bothering him for friendship. He still didn't know why. She was pretty and funny and they sat together during maths. Anne-Marie asked him out and he said yes. They met a couple of times in town and then they didn't speak for a while. He had no idea why at the time. Looking back, though, he realised how overwhelmed by her he'd been. He'd felt something for her. A kind of happy madness that he thought was love. And he told her so. He phoned her up one Sunday and told her he loved her.

When Sheldon found out, he probably thought it was the best thing that happened at school all year. David had been in the yard, alone, staring across the playing fields. Sheldon and his gang had found him.

"Oh, Anne-Marie! I love you!" Sheldon was yelling in a high-pitched voice across the yard. David saw kids turning and looking at him, kids he didn't know. He felt his heart pounding, his stomach squirming, his face warming. "I love you so much, Anne-Marie!" Sheldon had a hand on his chest and another in the air.

David walked towards him. "Shut up."

"I love you!"

"Shut the fuck up, Sheldon!"

"I love—" Sheldon wavered; his knees buckled then he dropped to all fours. David paused. Some of Sheldon's gang had moved forward. Sheldon got up and started for him. David hit him again. Sheldon's head twisted but he was ready this time and he refocused on David just before he hit him again.

Sheldon tried to hit him back but he could only wobble around like a toddler. David punched him again and again. Sheldon tripped over his own leg and fell. His gang backed off, staring.

Soon, most of the school was crowded around them. "Fight! Fight! Fight! Fight!" They sounded muffled and distant. David was straddling Sheldon, pummelling his face with both fists. Sheldon tried to guard himself but then he went limp and his head rocked from side to side as David swung his fists into it. All the while, David was sobbing: "Shut up, shut up."

The crowd had become silent and stared numbly at him until two teachers pulled him off and marched him towards the school building. He looked back at Sheldon. His face was a dirty red blob. David realised his hands were throbbing and he couldn't move his fingers. He'd only wanted him to shut up.

Now he was dreaming about him, his old friend. Sheldon was in a dark room but he could see him clearly. He was holding a dead baby, grinning.

David woke up, gasping, sobbing. He looked around but it was black everywhere. The dim fire snapped and fizzed. There was an owl somewhere near. He wriggled out of his sleeping bag and crawled out from under the tarp. Only the owl broke the silence. He felt for his torch and walked among the quiet trees. The moon was small and smiling through the branches. A haze obscured all but the brighter stars. His heart was calming but the dream image persisted and he noticed he was shaking. He found the moon again, stared at it, needing something to look at, something real. He rubbed his head, wiping away the spiders and flies.

There was a rustle to his left and he swung round. He made a sound like he was going to throw up. Among the trees was a Watcher, hooded and faceless. He could feel it staring at him – into him – then he did feel sick. He wanted to shout at the Watcher, tell it to fuck off, go away, but he couldn't speak. It stared at him in the silence and he stared back. The owl hooted again and the Watcher turned away. David felt its disgust, its disappointment.

Then the trees started talking about him again.

# TUESDAY

## 1

Gail put her coffee and two sweeteners in the mug Rob had bought her the last time they were in York. It was the first of three coffees she'd have today; any more than three and she usually went a bit wappy. The mug was thick earthenware with a gargoyle on the side; it was based on one of the waterspouts on the front of the Minster. She stared through the window at the aquamarine glass and blue brick of the neighbouring building. The Quantum Business Park at Longbenton was still being built. She could hear the muted sounds of power tools from the building site across the road. The wind blew little eddies of dust in the half-empty car park. She looked at the gurning face on the mug, ran her thumb over its bumpy features.

"Hello? Gail?" She spun her chair round and saw Lucy leaning over the partition between their two desks.

"Sorry, Luce," Gail said. "Miles away."

"You off to the bar?" Lucy handed her mug to her. "Same again?"

Gail took the two mugs into the kitchen. The room was empty and she took her phone out of her pocket, knowing before she saw the screen that there'd be no messages. She filled the mugs from the cistern and glugged milk into Lucy's mug. As she opened the fridge she heard the kitchen door open with its metallic whine. She swung around and Tom walked in. There was that same tight flutter in her upper abdomen.

"Morning," he called. Tom was a morning person.

"Tommy G," she muttered back.

"Good curry last night," he proclaimed, filling his mug with hot water. The tag of a herbal tea bag hung over the side of his mug.

"Yes, it was. Lush." She could feel herself flushing but she wasn't sure why. She'd only had three pints last night; surely she'd remember if she did anything regrettable.

"Do you want to do it again tonight?"

She picked up the mugs. "What?"

"Dinner. Come round to my place. I'll cook."

"I don't know." Her eyes fluttered. "I got some gammon out of the freezer this morning." She noticed that she was backing away from him, towards the door.

"Well, okay. The offer's there though, if you…"

"Okay. I'll think on it."

On the way back to her desk, she passed her line manager. "Morning, Steve."

"Gail. Where's Rob this morning?" Steve was the only person she knew who could mutter and shout at the same time.

"He's ill."

"Oh."

"Yeah. He came down with something yesterday morning so we had to cancel our day out."

"What's wrong with him?"

"D and V. Yeah. I was gutted. He's all right, though. Well he's not all right. He's in bed, on the toilet every twenty minutes."

Steve nodded. "You don't feel ill, do you?"

"No, I'm fine."

"Well if you start feeling sick just get yourself home. Don't want the entire office infected."

"Roger that."

Back at her desk she checked her emails and sipped her coffee. She sat back and stared across the office, through the windows on the opposite side of the building. The same drab half-buildings beyond. Marcus from HR was standing near the water cooler talking to one of the new girls. They both looked at her then realised she was looking back. They chatted to each other for a moment longer then walked away.

She took another sip of coffee. The gargoyle gave her its sinister grin. Her eyes glazed. At one time, they were more carefree, less serious. The blurry times at the flat at the end of the nineties – their half-lost decade – when he always seemed to be buying her flowers. Then back to their first date at the almost empty pub in Rusholme. His hazel eyes, the long brown hair, always clean and pulled back in a ponytail. He was slimmer then. And grungier, like he didn't care. Because he didn't. He was the easiest person to talk to she knew. He had a soothing confidence about him. He calmed her, cushioned the blows.

These days he was more irritable, quick to anger. She could sense a bitter rage simmering underneath his outward serenity. At times, she felt uncomfortable around him; at others, outright scared. The Rob she used to know was slowly leaving her. And she didn't know why.

She sipped her coffee again and guilt welled up inside her. She wanted to go to Tom's tonight but she knew she shouldn't. But he was only a friend; nothing would happen. Maybe after a few looseners, she'd open up to him. About Rob.


## 2


Tidying wasn't Fraser's favourite thing. The boy did it mostly, under the Boss' direction. But the boy wasn't available. He was being detained.

The kitchen was easy enough. A place for everything. After you use something, put it away.

The snug, however, was a challenge. It was where something new was put until it turned into something old. The room used to be his favourite – a quiet place where he could read, or listen to the radio or Frank. But now it was a store room and he had no desire to spend time there even if he could. Besides, he preferred the Big Room. His chair was comfortable and the window was large with a good view of the fields towards town.

He'd been meaning to tidy the snug for a while now but he knew there were things in there he'd rather not re-find. He moved boxes and bags to create a path. The further into the room he got, the older it all became. Bills, clothes, police training material, files with his school work. All his old vinyl records that he'd replaced with CDs. Maybe some of those were worth something. He didn't know why he'd been keeping hold of the stuff. It would be at least two trips to the charity shop and the tip.

A photograph album.

He tried to pull it off the shelf with two fingers but it was tight between her old art books. He tipped it back and tried again. The album was heavy. He knew what he'd find inside it. He shouldn't open it but he was here now and he was holding it. How would he react to all the memories? He held the album by its spine and pulled open the cover. It made a sticky sound. The first two pictures were mounted behind yellowed plastic. The bride alone. The bride with her late father. He tutted and didn't know why. The stiff page made the same sticky sound. Another four photos, these of the bride and her mum (the sour cunt) and dad and her sister. She was a wee doll, Fiona, in her day. Another page. The groom with his moustache and hired penguin suit. The memory forced a smile. He turned the pages quicker, past relatives he'd not seen for years and some he'd probably never see again.

He stopped at the first photo of the boy. Not a week old. He found himself staring at it. His eyes filled and the image blurred. He turned more pages, watching the boy grow up, the changing hairstyles, the changing seasons. He stopped again at a picture of the boy in Spain, maybe a year before she left. He was standing on one hip at the side of the swimming pool, trying to hold a huge beach ball under one arm and shading his eyes from the afternoon sun. Fraser could feel the heat on the back of his head, remembered glancing down at the boy's wee trunks as he looked through the viewfinder. He'd told the boy to say cheese then his lips had pulled away from his teeth and his eyes tightened.

Fraser stroked his cock through his sweat pants. He placed the album on some stacked boxes, gently, like it was fragile, sacred. He pulled his sweatpants and shorts over his erection and started massaging the tip. He heard the wind bumping against the window, nothing else. A whispered moan escaped. The boy was still beautiful but back then he was perfect. The blond hair, the pale skin. Angelic. He barged the sudden thought of Jesus and the Virgin Mary from his mind, concentrated on the boy.

He heard the door creak and his heart lurched. He jerked his head round. The boy was standing in the doorway, spying on him. Fraser snatched at his pants. "Get back to your room," he blurted. "You little cunt."

His voice reverberated in the hallway. The boy disappeared. "Fuck," Fraser hissed and he felt his face redden like he was a naughty schoolboy. His erection relaxed. The wee fucker was in for it now.

### 3

The map showed a drove road leading north from the head of Loch Merkland. It would be easier on the feet, flat and hopefully deserted. To get to it, though, he would have to cross the A-road that ran northwest across Sutherland.

He followed the contours of the valley, watching and listening as he broke the cover of the trees. As he reached the head of the valley he could see the peak of Ben More Assynt off to the west.

His path curved round to the east, finding the lowest contours, following the water. Through a knot of rocky outcrops at the head of Loch Merkland. The land dropped down to the road. He stood sniffing and panting, scanning the line of cars that stood further up the valley. Workmen scurried round a huge yellow earthmover and the tiny red dot of a traffic light. A high dry-stone wall bounded the far side of the road until the opening for the drove road. "Shit."

David scrambled over rocks and scree onto rough grass below. A brisk wind blew from across the valley and as he thrust his hands into his pockets he saw the lights change. The line of traffic slid towards him and he dropped to his haunches. The traffic disappeared towards the loch and he continued down towards the road. A few more cars straggled along and he paused until they too faded away. Another line was forming back at the lights. He skipped over long, coarse grass that pulsated in the wind. He wanted to cross the road as near to the loch as possible, closer to the drove road.

The line of traffic was getting longer. David started getting a sick feeling in his stomach and the tops of his thighs felt queasy. "I'll have to time it right." He saw the lights change and the cars and buses and motor homes moved forward. He found a dip in the land and crouched there, listening to the traffic as it swished by. When the last stragglers had gone he sprang up and almost broke into a run as the land flattened out. Soon though it turned boggy and his progress slowed. The white tufts of cotton grass dotted the land. A new line of traffic was forming at the lights.

David flailed his arms, trying to keep balance on the unyielding ground, and became conscious of being seen. He slowed even further, almost tiptoeing. But he was almost at the road now. The loch lay like a black slug under the mountains. The lights had not changed yet and he weighed up his chances of getting to the drove road before the traffic passed. He scanned between the lights and his target. "Nowhere to hide." He had to chance it. The tarmac was welcome relief after the uneven hillside and the spongy bog. He skipped along, twisting round towards the green dot. He could see the entrance of the drove road. He looked back. Cars were moving towards him. "Fuck." He sped up and then thought better of it: as far as they were concerned, he was just any other rambler. "Keep walking." He pulled his hood up. The noise was getting louder behind. He tried to relax and look like any other rambler. The first car passed him after pipping its horn. "Keep walking." David left the road for the grassy verge, taking care not to get too near to the drainage ditch. The grass here was grimy with road filth. He stared at the horizon, self-conscious, feeling eyes on him. Car after car grated past. A coach rumbled by, towering over him. He felt clammy in its shadow. "Keep walking." The queasy feeling in his thighs was spreading to his groin and knees. He felt his feet speeding up again.

He couldn't help it: his head just turned to the right on its own. As he did an estate car stuffed with camping gear drove by. Among the sleeping bags, stoves and plastic tennis rackets, a boy of about seven with curly hair was squeezed up against the window. His eyes met David's. He wondered why the boy's hair was blond and his eyes were brown. The boy didn't look away so David had to. He looked for the drove road. Nearby, the wall ran away from the road. He hopped down into the drainage ditch and his boot sank into the mud. But then he was clawing up the other side and striding towards the wall. "Don't look back now." He'd been seen. "Don't look back." He imagined the cars skidding to a halt and the drivers running after him. But soon the noise died down and there was only the sound of the breeze and a lark warbling somewhere over the heath.

When he stepped onto the stony drove road he allowed himself to peek back. He let the road slip behind and felt his heart relaxing. He looked up at the hillside to a small plantation where he'd camp tonight. In the morning the drove road would take him halfway to Tongue, where he would follow the coast east to Thurso.

"Thurso. Thurso."

## 4

The handsome Victorian stone terraces of Muirend glowed red in the early evening sun. A shower had just passed and dark grey clouds hung behind the houses and trees.

Rob took his overnight bag out of the boot and walked along the pavement, craning his neck as he looked for Phil's house. With their large sash windows, chunky privet hedges and small trees in long gardens, all the houses here looked similar. At some distance above the swish of the traffic, a car horn played the first few notes of "Dixie". For a moment, he was transported to his own childhood streets and he laughed to himself.

He recognised Phil's house by the privet arch over the tall iron gate. Knocking on the door, he heard the Rolling Stones through a window above and he smiled again. He thought of the drunken arguments he'd had with Phil when they were younger, back in Leeds; he still thought Phil's musical education needed work.

Phil's wife answered the door.

"Rachel! How the devil are you?"

"Great," she replied in her diluted Glaswegian.

"You got my message."

"Yes," she sighed, rolling her eyes in mock exasperation, although Rob knew she was genuinely annoyed.

"Did you miss me?"

She rolled her eyes again and swung the door wide. "Come in, Rob. Shoes off." She took his bag, backed up a few steps across the glossy parquet floor and dumped it next to the wall. "You had a good day?"

"Not bad, not bad," he said, rubbing his palms. "Phil in?"

"Mmm?"

"Where's Phil?"

"Oh, he's upstairs, getting changed. He's only just got in."

"I could do with a shower myself, actually. It's been a bit sticky today. Bit moist." He grinned and clapped once.

"Has it?" she sighed and retreated towards the kitchen.

"Eh?"

Phil bounded down the stairs. "Now then, buggerlugs."

"Now then." They shook hands, smiling.

"What's for tea? I'm starving."

"Rude pig."

"Well I haven't eaten since breakfast."

"Come through." They followed Rachel down the hall. "We thought we'd get a takeaway. Due to the change of plans." The large kitchen was shaded behind the angry receding clouds.

Phil slid up to the fridge. "Beer?"

"Is the bear a Catholic?"

Phil gave a short, sharp laugh, then: "Does the Pope shit in the woods?" He opened two bottles and handed the first to Rob. They knocked them together. "Chin-chin," Phil said.

"Up yours." Rob looked at Rachel. She stood at the other side of the farmhouse table, hugging a large glass of white wine. "And yours, Rachel. Good health, I mean." He leaned over, holding out his bottle. She unfolded her arms and clonked it with her glass. They all took a drink together and stood there for a moment that seemed to last longer than it should.

## 5

"Something smells nice," Gail called out. She was sitting on Tom's hard white sofa. It was more like an upholstered school bench. She wanted to sit back but she had to sit upright with her knees together and her toes overlapping. Tom's risotto had been delicious: real home-made chicken stock and wild mushrooms. But there was too much and now she was bloated. He hadn't heard her from the kitchen and her glass was nearly empty so she stood up.

She felt her eyes flickering as she said: "Something smells nice."

Tom was washing up. The sleeves of his black fitted shirt were neatly rolled up to the elbows. "Oh it's just a candle. I like to put one on after eating. Gets rid of food odours."

"You're all man, aren't you?" she said and Tom laughed. She shook her empty bottle at him. "Any more...?" He dried his hands and waltzed over to the fridge, which wasn't quite big enough to walk into. He grabbed a bottle and took the top off with a wall-mounted opener. The top fell into a small, dedicated bin. He took her glass. "Ice, madam?"

"No. I'm all right."

"I know that but do you want any ice?"

She giggled and shook her head. He poured the cider. "I need a wee."

"Good to know. I'll take this in for you."

She climbed the narrow staircase to the bathroom and sneaked into Tom's bedroom on the way. It was like a hotel room. There was nothing superfluous: everything had a purpose and a place. There was even a narrow over-sheet at the foot of the bed if he felt like doing something cavalier like having five minutes after work and didn't want to take his shoes off. She smiled and soft-footed over to the tall window. She looked across rows of terraced houses, their chimneys like gravestones, throwing long shadows in the reddening dusk. A telephone wire swung in the wind. She looked down at the street and watched a carrier bag dancing in an eddy behind a parked car.

A feeling like nausea rose through her chest and into her throat. Her eyes brimmed. She stepped away from the window, dabbing her tears, and noticed that she'd left the greasy print of her forehead and nose on the window. She gathered her cuff in her hand and wiped it but it just smeared. Tears trickled down the edge of her nose and gathered under her chin. Her face screwed up and she frantically scrubbed the window. Now she was softly sobbing.

"Gail?" Tom called from downstairs. "You all right?"

"Yeah!" she gurgled. "Just washing my hands." She heard him climbing the stairs and then he was in the doorway.

"What's wrong?"

She swung around, hunched over, her sleeve still in her hand. "I muckied your window." He walked towards her and there was no escape. His arms enveloped her and she brought her hands up. Then she was sobbing into his chest and he was saying "Shh". He felt firm and warm, like her bed. Her hands fell and wrapped around his waist. He squeezed her gently, pulling her further in. He was letting her cry everything out wordlessly and he would stay there for as long as it took. She thought about the mess she was making of his shirt.

"You can stay here tonight if you want," he whispered. "In the spare bedroom."

She looked up at him and thought about what she must look like. She nodded and sniffed. "He doesn't love me anymore."

"I don't think—"

"There's no affection. I go to hug him and it's like hugging a sack of spuds." She sniffed, then laughed. "That was the first real hug I've had for ages." Tom unwrapped his arms and held her gently by the shoulders. "There's no trust," she said. "On either side. We don't talk to each other anymore. Not about the serious stuff." She sniffed again and couldn't help wiping her nose on her sleeve. "I think he might've gone off with another woman. For good."

"I don't think he has. He'll be in touch. If it's what it sounds like, he just needs some time to himself. He'll phone you soon. Just wait and see."

Tom showed her the spare room. It was a smaller version of his room. She slept on top of the sheets in her clothes and woke up in the same position.

## 6

He was dreaming about Sheldon again. The baby was blue and floppy. Sheldon was grinning. He'd picked up the baby to show David.

He awoke with a loud moan and listened to the swaying, whispering pines. Like a distant beach. The wind had blown the cloud cover away and he rubbed his nose warm, rubbed his head. The spiders were getting worse now. And tonight, as the sun was setting, he saw black things flying between the trees. They might have been small, beakless birds or huge flies, like clegs; he couldn't tell. The moon grinned at him like Sheldon.

He put the memories out of his head with hard slaps to his scalp and cheek. He was well aware that all this time spent alone wasn't doing his head any good. He missed the company of the people he knew, although they would all be part of the effort to track him down now. Maybe his mother was immune to it, though. She'd be worried about him, in spite of everything. He might not see her again. He thought he might phone her when he got to Thurso. The other day was the last time he'd seen her. Friday afternoon, was it? He was working on his Millennium Falcon model, listening to Nine Inch Nails.

"I've brought you some grapefruit juice," she said, turning the music down. She tidied up around him. She always tidied and washed up when she came, whether he wanted her to or not.

"Is it pink?"

"Aye, it's pink." She took some empty glasses into the kitchen. The house belonged to his dad: a little stone semi in Drummond, near the Ness. A small living room and a smaller kitchen with oak flooring. It was cosy but big enough for his needs and it was within walking distance of work and he didn't have to pay any rent. It was his dad's way of paying him off.

"How's Dad?" He always asked the question like it was a chore.

"Aye, he's all right." Mum always sounded enthusiastic when she answered. "I haven't seen him for a few days." She handed him a pint of squash. "How did your fishing go?"

"All right."

"Have you taken your pills today?"

"Mum! I've told you before! Don't treat me like a fucking baby!" It was just one time.

"David. Don't speak to me like that." She sounded as disappointed as she always did when he spoke to her like that. "I'm your mother. It's my job to worry about you." She plumped up some cushions. "No matter how old you get."

"Yes, yes."

Just one time. He'd stopped taking his meds because of the side effects: the dizziness, the headaches, the dry mouth, the nausea, the stomach pain, the constipation, the sweating, the fact he couldn't come anymore no matter how hard he tried. And the fucking weird dreams. Not all at once, but he'd had the lot at one time or another. This particular time, he'd had a headache that lasted more than a week and he felt like he was on a fishing boat in the middle of the North Sea in a winter storm. So he'd stopped taking the pills and he'd lied to his mum.

"Have you eaten?"

"Yes. No."

"What have you got?"

"Erm, a lasagne I think."

"I'll bake you an apple crumble for the weekend. If you behave yourself." He didn't smile. "I didn't have time today."

She started telling him something about his sister's love life but he stopped listening. The Millennium Falcon was tougher than he'd expected. He was wishing he had small hands like a girl. He was trying to glue the gun turret in place and it was proving to be a right old bastard. He rose up from the depths of his concentration to hear the phone ringing. Mum was saying: "I tell you, she can't tell a fart from a yawn, that girl." She looked at the phone. "You can answer that if you want."

"It'll be no one I know."

The phone had kept ringing. Mum had disappeared upstairs somewhere and David had turned the volume back up. "Big Man with a Big Gun" had just given way to "A Warm Place".

Now he sat back against a tree, staring at the moon and polishing the compass lid with his thumb. David liked his mum. "She's the only one that mattered, really." He knew she'd be worried.

## 7

The front room – or drawing room, as Rachel called it – was too large, with empty oak flooring amid the sparse furniture. A high ceiling and bare walls. The large bay window was speckled with rain, backlit by the orange glow from the street. The room was tastefully done with neutral colours. A bit like Phil's life.

Rob and Phil sat on a brown leather sofa. Rachel was sprawled on another, holding her half-empty glass by the stem. The television babbled softly: some reality show that Rob had never seen. He and Phil shared a road atlas.

"There won't be anywhere for you to get a decent curry over the next few days, I reckon," Phil said.

"Not even in Thurso?"

"Don't know. Maybe Wick. Have you ever been to Thurso, Babe?" Rachel seemed to find it a challenge to figure out who had spoken to her.

Rob said: "I've told you before, Phil. Stop calling me that," and smiled at Rachel. "Eh?" She didn't smile back. Her programme was much more entertaining than him. Phil laughed, even though it was maybe the third time Rob had made the joke.

That was one of the reasons he liked Phil, since their school days: he always laughed at his jokes.

"No," Rachel said. "Furthest I've been is Inverness." Beyond the slight slur, her accent was thicker. She lay on her side, propping herself up on the soft arm of the sofa. Her upper leg was bent and she wiggled and stretched her bare, white toes. In the dusky light, Rob caught the round bulge between her legs, imagined it red and swollen, like a ripe pomegranate.

"So you're going up the Trossachs," Phil said, taking the map.

"Uh?"

"Then over to Pitlochry?"

"Oh, yeah. Then north. Till there's nowhere else to go, I suppose."

"There's a good distillery there. Pitlochry. And you'll need to go to Glen Nevis if you get over that way." He studied the map up close.

"Maybe." Rob glanced at the television. He spoke to Rachel: "What's this shite you're watching, anyway?" Again she swung her head round and blew a little raspberry that made him grin. "You know, we live in a country where most people's main concern is whether Paris Hilton wants to have her arsehole bleached." Phil blurted out another wet laugh. "Eh?" Rachel was oblivious, or pretended to be. "Is this the one in Newcastle?" He feigned complete ignorance of the programme.

"Aye," she said, glassy-eyed.

"Oh dear."

"How long have you been in Newcastle now,

Robbo?" Phil said, still looking at the map.

"Twelve years? Fourteen. Jesus. Fourteen years. Ninety-eight, I moved up there. Or down there. Whichever."

"Do you still keep in touch with the lads?" He closed the map and took a swig from his bottle.

"No," Rob said, "I haven't been back for ages."

"Me neither. Well, I go down at Christmas but only to see the family. What about that flat you had? That was a right weekend when we came down to stay that time."

"In Leeds?"

"No, Newcastle."

"Oh, yeah. When you tried to climb that lamp-post?"

Phil laughed silently, tears welling. "I was so pissed."

"And her," nodding towards Rachel. "With that dwarf." Phil's head fell back and he made a sound almost like a scream.

"Who's 'her'? The cat's mother?" Rachel called out, not taking her eyes off the television.

Phil carried on reminiscing but Rob was drifting off, staring at the screen. They had been good times at that flat. When they were younger and less serious about life. Or was it that, now, they were more resigned to life? In those days, they never seemed to be able to leave each other alone. As soon as he came in from work she seemed to always be there ready to jump and clamp her legs around him. They would stand there in the poky little hallway, with their trousers round their ankles, her with her palms and ear against the wall as if listening to the neighbours arguing.

He smiled then started, refocusing his eyes. He realised he'd been twisting his wedding ring. He took another big mouthful of lager. It was warm now.

Phil's head had slumped back and nestled in the soft leather. His mouth lolled open and he soon started to snore. Rachel scowled at him. "Phil! You're not sleeping there again. Go to bed!" She puffed and tottered to her feet, still holding her glass. Her auburn hair half-covered her face as she minced over to Phil. "Wake up, Phil." She pushed his shoulder. "Wake up, you smelly bastard." Rob loved the way she said her esses like Sean Connery when she was drunk.

Phil lifted his head and made a noise that seemed to amalgamate all five vowels. He looked around, trying to find who had woken him up. "Myrrh."

"It's time for bed, Big Man," Rob said, standing. He helped Rachel get Phil to his feet.

Phil slowly wrapped his arms around his friend. "Love you, you big bugger."

"I love you too." Rob patted his back and looked at Rachel over his shoulder. She had a hand on Phil's side, as much to steady herself than him. Rob moved his hand down and their fingers touched. She felt hard and cold and she quickly moved her hand away. "Sorry," he called, like it was an accident. "Come on, Big Man."

"I'll be right," Rachel said as Phil swung around and hung his arm over her shoulder.

"Yeah, I'll be all right," Phil said. "You stay up. Get what you want out of the fridge. Bacon and eggs for breakfast. Mushrooms. We have mushrooms. Nighty night." He lurched towards the open door into the darkness of the hallway. Rachel followed him to turn all the lights on and then came back to pick up the empties. Phil slowly climbed the stairs, grabbing the bannister with each step. He saw Rob watching and eventually brought his finger to his lips. "Shh." Rob laughed and sat down again, watched Phil disappear.

"I'll wash up, I think," Rachel said.

"I'll have another…" He waved his bottle. "If you're going into the kitchen."

"Cheeky." She took the bottle and wriggled through the door. He smiled and felt his cock squirm. He stared at the television for a long time, not watching, not listening. Then he stood and padded through the door, turning the hallway lights off as he made towards the kitchen.

Rachel was stood with her hands in the sink. Her paisley top buttoned up the back and the hem curved apart at the bottom, showing a pale triangle of skin above the magnificent curve of her jeans. Rob saw an opened bottle beside her on the worktop. He picked it up and sipped from it. "Hello", he grinned.

She turned her head, her hair still wild and covering one eye. "What are you up to?" She gave a coy smirk and her nostrils flared. Rob stared at the thin lips and the deep, narrow philtrum above. He took another sip and put the bottle down, looking down at the small, naked patch of skin. He ran his fingertips over it. "Rob." She pulled her hands out of the sink. Rob twisted her round, looping an arm round her waist and throwing another over her shoulder. Rachel screwed up her arms like a boxer covering up. Rob felt her cool, wet fists on his chest, heard the bubbles fizzing there. He planted his mouth on hers and their teeth clashed. He felt his stubble against her soft chin. She felt warm and tacky and she tasted of wine. "Get off!" she yelled and pushed him away. He stepped back.

"I thought—"

"What the fuck are you doing?" she hissed.

"I was kissing you."

"I'm married. To your best mate."

He stepped forward again. "Come on. For old times' sake."

"Old times? That was one time. We were drunk."

"What? Like now?"

"Drunker. And I was in a different place then."

"Oh."

"I'm happier now. We're both happier. Look. I don't even fancy you."

"Yeah, right. I've seen the way you've been looking at me all night."

"The way you've been looking at me all night." She picked up a tea towel, wrung her hands. "I've got work in the morning. Your room's at the top of the stairs."

"Fuck that." He searched the room for his car keys, found them next to the back door. He grabbed them and tried the door but it was locked.

"Rob. Don't even think about driving anywhere." He was striding across the kitchen towards the hallway and the front door. Rachel followed him.

"Let's just forget about it. Please, Rob. Don't go."

Rob slammed the door shut. He swung the gate open and strode to his car. A young couple walked past, all arms. "Fuck it!" he spat and the couple moved away. He pressed the button on his key fob and the car chirruped. It took him an aeon to get the key in the ignition. He calmed himself and twisted the key. The radio blared out. "Ruby Tuesday". He told Mick Jagger to Fuck Off and jabbed the radio off. Then he thumped the steering wheel until his knuckles ached, remembering that he'd forgotten his overnight bag.

## 8

"You know it's for your own good, don't you?"

Ali stood next to the kitchen table, staring at the clock on the oven. It said 19:32 in green. The 2 changed to a 3 as he watched the two dots blinking. Miss Palmer had told them that was called a colon. He made soft clicks with his tongue in time with it.

"What have I said about answering when I ask you a direct question, laddie?"

"I thought—"

"Not a rhetorical question. You know what a rhetorical question is. Don't think you can play games with me, boy. I always win."

"Sorry, Father."

"Well?"

"Aye, Father. I know it's for my own good." He started tapping the table top, double timing the oven clock. The yellowness of the pine: it wasn't right, it wasn't natural. All the other wood in the kitchen was the same sickly yellow pine. The cupboard doors, the drawers, the dresser, the skirting boards. He always felt queasy in the kitchen.

"Good. I'm the one who has to raise you. To teach you right from wrong. After all, it's your fault your mum died." Dad had told him this before. He wasn't sure if it was true or not. Ali felt his throat tighten but he willed the tears back. It wasn't good to cry in front of Dad. "And stop your fucking tapping."

Ali took a step back from the table and tapped the back of his fingers. The wind was making the house creak. Frank Sinatra was singing in the living room. Dad had made a CD with nothing but "My Kind of Town" on it. Ali hated it.

"Aye, Father."

"Good. It's well that you understand."

"Father, what have I done wrong?"

"You know what you've done wrong, laddie." Dad lifted the back of the chair as he stood. He side-stepped to the dresser, steadying himself on the table with his fingertips. Everything in the drawer shifted as he opened it. When he turned, he was holding his tack hammer. Ali felt everything slump: his insides, his shoulders, his legs. He couldn't help taking a step back. "Step up to the table, laddie."

"Father."

"Put your palms on the table."

"Please, Father." Dad came to the corner of the table, towering over him. Ali could smell him: the booze and the sweat.

"What have I done wrong, Father?" He looked at the hammer. It was old and blackened.

"You don't want to say that again." Dad was working his fingers over the handle, trying to find the best grip.

"Father, I won't do it again."

"See, you say that every time. Palm." Ali made loose fists and felt the sticky warmth of his hands. He raised his hand towards the table. "Your left one. We want you to be able to write when you go back to school. Agreed?" Ali raised his other hand and Dad grabbed his wrist. His fingers were cold and strong. He squeezed harder and Ali couldn't help crying out. Dad slapped his palm on the table top and raised his hammer to his shoulder.

# WEDNESDAY

## 1

From the roundabout at Aberfoyle the road wound up the hillside, through dense bracken and heather, climbing up to a shallow saddle of rock between two peaks before dropping down into the next glen. At Brig o' Turk Rob got stuck behind a coach. "Fuck it," he hissed, but the driver pulled over. He passed and flashed his hazard lights a few times in thanks and he followed the road down to Kilmahog, then left and northward. Past long lochs trapped between god-like massifs, past villages that seemed no more than clusters of B&Bs, gift shops, pubs and visitor centres.

At Killin the traffic slowed and he noticed a slim,

pretty girl of seventeen or eighteen standing at a bus shelter. "All right, sweetheart?" he called as he glided past.

"Fuck off," she answered. He laughed and drove on. Diana said something. She was friendly enough; she had a slightly patronising tone that Rob didn't have much time for but, going on the voice alone, she'd have probably got it.

"I don't know why you're so chirpy, anyway. All you get to do all day is give me directions." He glanced down at the screen and the little car creeping along the little road. "You don't get to look at all this scenery."

"Ahead, keep left."

"Yeah, whatever."

The road pitched and yawed along the north shore of Loch Tay, overshadowed by vast, hulking masses of rock. He began singing along with Prince again. At Kenmore he drove over the narrow bridge at the mouth of the loch and gave an "Aaaah" as he saw clouds and pines tumbling down the northern hillsides into the violet water.

When he reached Pitlochry he drove slowly along the main street and scanned for a hotel. The town seemed more lived in than the earlier villages. He parked up and checked his phone: texts and missed calls from Gail and a text from Phil. He ignored that too. He booked into the Tummel View Hotel, which served as one of the golf clubs in town. He took a shower then followed the brown signs up the hillside to the smallest distillery in Scotland. At the ticket office, he found himself alone with a young blonde –

maybe twenty-two – in a tartan miniskirt.

He bought his ticket then said in his best Scottish accent: "You're a pretty wee lassie, very wee."

"Well, you know what they say," she retorted with a practised smile. "The smaller the still, the finer the whisky."

He gave a short laugh. "I bet they do. I bet they do." He gave up with the accent: "I'm staying at the Tummel View, if you fancy a drink. Later."

Still smiling: "I don't think my boyfriend would be too happy about that."

"He can come too."

"No, thanks," she laughed.

"No harm in trying."

He walked out into the yard outside the ticket office. It was still early. He'd woken up about an hour after dawn with a pounding head and a shitty mouth. He'd rubbed sleep from his eyes and walked back to Phil's house for his bag. He cringed at the prospect of having to knock on the door. Instead, he opened the gate at the back, hoping the door would be unlocked. He found the bag next to the steps.

After taking the car to a drive-through for one of the worst breakfasts he'd ever had, he'd driven north through a waking Glasgow and a fine, soft drizzle and into the Trossachs under a defiant sun.

Here now the rain had returned and the sky was a uniform milky grey.

The tour started with a tasting. Rob cringed as the tour guide rallied everyone: it was the girl from the ticket office. She led everyone into a large room with round tables and invited them to take a seat. There was a tulip-shaped glass in front of him – Rob recalled that it was called a snifter – and the blonde guide drifted around the room with a bottle, giving everyone a dram.

She took them through the process of tasting: swirling the whisky in the snifter and then smelling. She said it had an estery quality and one might detect dried fruit notes, but Rob thought it just smelled of whisky. He scanned the room, twisting his wedding ring. No-one was looking so he necked the dram, working his mouth and cheeks as the liquid burned his chest. "Very clever finish," he said, perhaps a bit too loudly as the Germans next to him gave him a quick glare.

"...on the palate," the guide was saying, "due to the fact that this particular whisky was aged in a sherry cask, you might detect spicy vanilla notes." She sounded as if she was reading it from a book for the first time. Rob suspected the closest she'd come to tasting whisky was sucking on a novelty condom her boyfriend had bought in the pub toilets while she was getting the alcopops in.

"Its arrogance amuses me," he exclaimed. The Germans weren't the only ones to glare at him this time. The guide paused for a while then carried on talking to the people who were actually interested.

He got to keep the snifter and he carried it round the rest of the tour: into the shed where they did the ageing, which smelled of whisky, and to the place where the actual distilling took place, which also smelled of whisky. There were two greenish, copper pot stills in a little whitewashed shed and a raised gangway so that enthusiasts could take photos from every angle.

Rob saw a sign for the tasting bar and strode into the room with his snifter held high. "What do you recommend?"

The barman wore the same tartan as the tour guide. "Well, sir, it depends what you're after. Would you like peaty, fruity or floral?"

"Give me peaty." He was looking for a stool so he could get comfortable but there wasn't one.

"Sure." He picked up a bottle. "This one is aged fifteen years. Smells like a hospital, tastes like heaven."

"Sold!" Rob said. He could feel his cheeks were still flushed from the earlier dram.

The barman placed the snifter down as if it were a family heirloom. "Note the oily quality of the whisky as you swirl it."

Rob held the glass to the light and then necked it. "What else you got?"

The barman gave a disapproving frown. "Lingers on the palate, that one, sir. Perhaps you might have a wee drop of water before your next taste."

"Have you got one that tastes like my grandfather's old study used to smell?" He plonked the snifter on the bar.

"Well…"

"What about that one? That's a nice colour."

"That one is our rarest whisky, sir. It's twenty-one years old and it has a price tag to reflect that."

Rob glared at him for a second. "That's a coincidence. I'm twenty-one today. I'll have a wee dram of that, by the way."

He was asked to leave after he called the barman a specky, bald cunt in the style of Rab C Nesbitt.

## 2

Another cheese and pickle sandwich. Fraser sucked on his bottle of lager after buttering the bread then looked through the kitchen window at the drizzle. He cut the cheese thick. The boy needed some meat on his bones, make him a wee bit more cuddly. He remembered the incident in the study and he dropped the knife and took another swig. He looked at the bottle, finished it.

Was he too hard on the boy? But he was his sole guardian and the boy was his ward.

The kitchen door squeaked open and the boy floated in like a ghost. His tee shirt was crumpled: he must've slept in it. He looked at the floor as he walked.

"Good of you to join us," Fraser sang. The boy didn't respond, sat at the table. Fraser smeared the pickle into the buttered bread and slapped the slice onto the cheese. He took the boy's lunch over to the table and placed it before him.

The boy looked at the sandwich. "Thank you, Father." He looked tiny.

"No bother." He saw the boy turn his head towards him. He didn't lift it. He was glancing at his crotch. Fraser realised his sweat pants might not be as clean as when he put them on this morning. "What the fuck are you looking at, boy?"

"Nothing, Father."

"Nothing, Father. Well keep your eyes on what you're doing. Agreed? It's your favourite: cheese and pickle." Fraser turned and brought back a glass of barley water: another treat. "What have you been up to all morning? Anything exciting?"

"I was just in bed, Father. Reading."

"You'll be staying in today?" He opened another bottle. "With this rain." The bin lid clanged when he stepped on the pedal. He dropped the bottle top from a height like a sorcerer adding something weird to his cauldron.

"Aye, Father."

"Well, I'll be in the Big Room most of the day." He put the bread back in the bread bin. "Don't be making too much noise; I might drop off this afternoon." He opened the fridge and put the cheese and the butter and the pickle back in. "Get plenty of rest."

### 3

The beer garden was behind the hotel, next to the car park. The eighteenth hole was just over the fence and Rob watched the golfers with a half-amused smirk. Little clusters of pine dotted the fairway. He wondered if they'd been planted there or if they'd cut most of the others down.

He had just stuffed a tuna sandwich into his mouth and was working on his chips and onion rings. He regretted putting too much vinegar on the chips but the onion rings were good. Not too greasy.

The high sun was trying to dissolve a stubborn haze. Before him there were three empties, and two-thirds that was getting warmer by the minute. It was a good bar: they had eight real ales, most of them local, and he intended to sample them all; a straight gallon before an afternoon snooze. He picked up his glass and tried to ignore the musty odour it gave off, took a couple of gulps. He placed it back down and stared at the suds clinging to the sides of the glass.

He recalled the time they'd dog-sat for Gail's friend, Alice. She'd gone to Skiathos for a week and thought it'd be easier to palm the dog off on them than put it in kennels. A big, daft poodle called Lucy. They took Lucy for a walk on the Saturday in High Park Wood. A day much like today: a soft, fine drizzle that gave way to haze then the sun burning through. They found themselves off the gravel path and in dense birches; ambled arm in arm, weaving through the trees, the dog bouncing up and down as if it had never been for a walk before.

Rob's hand dropped down to her hips and then further. He slipped it between her thighs and felt the heat there. They fucked standing up, she with her shoulder against a tree while he kept lookout and the dog bounded around. He had to keep palming the dog away and it went lolloping through the trees, circling them and barking.

"Shut the fuck up," he hissed, and all the time Gail laughing and moaning. They'd done it outside a few times before and this time it was fun but it didn't seem to be as exciting. They came together as they often did and they pulled their jeans back on and sat arm in arm under the tree. "I love you, Gooey," he panted.

She came in close, trying to touch as much of him as she could, squirming, kissing his cheek. "I love you too, Kirk Hammerton."

"Will you marry me?" And she cried softly and they took the dog home and they spent the rest of the afternoon and night in bed.

That was the last time things like that happened. Even before the wedding, the sex had started to trail off. And he still didn't know why. Maybe that was the problem. Gail probably knew exactly why. They'd just have to have a long adult discussion about their feelings when he got back, after she started talking to him again due to him fucking off to Scotland for a week without telling her. He drove the thought of the future argument from his mind.

He finished his pint and was about to get up. A group of golfers, some young, others middle-aged, were finding their cars. Despite the age gaps they all seemed to know each other. He stood up and saw that they all wore garish argyle jumpers and tweed plus fours. Whether they were trying to be ironic or not, they looked like twats. Some of them spoke with loud southern accents but one of the older men sounded like he was from Yorkshire. He shouted to one of the younger ones: "Blair, can you take my stuff to the car? Need to wet the old brogues."

"Sure. Which is it?"

"The gold one."

Rob scanned the car park for his car. "That's not gold. It's metallic beige." Most of the crowd looked over, and a couple of drinkers in the beer garden. "Eh?" A couple tittered and then the crowd dispersed. Rob heard the word "prick" mentioned as he went inside to the bar, grinning.

## 4

Gail had work to do but her head still felt like cotton wool from last night. It was stuffy in the office. Someone had opened a window and building site noises drifted up: drilling, sawing, music. She looked up at the grey, muted stillness outside and her eyes defocused.

They'd met at a club called Metropolis near the campus when he was in his final year of English and she was in her second year. A Thursday – it must've been Thursday because it was Bummed, the night when they played nothing but Manchester bands. He always said that he'd bumped into her, but she remembered it was the other way round. They were both a bit drunk; she was standing in front of him at the bar and she turned around and spilled half of her cider down him.

They had to shout at each other above the New Order (or maybe The Smiths). She had to tiptoe to shout in his ear and have her ear shouted into. She remembered how normal it felt to hold onto his shoulder to steady herself.

She couldn't remember what they talked about, just that they laughed a lot. She did recall clearly that "Love Will Tear Us Apart" was playing as they walked out of the club into the dry, cold night. They tottered and laughed towards her house and he said: "Do you fancy me, then, or what?"

She stopped under the rusty orange glow of a street lamp and took his hand. They turned to each other, their cold breaths curling around them. She looked up into his eyes.

"Yes. I do, actually." And then she threw an arm around his neck and lifted herself and kissed him messily on the lips. They got to her door and he kissed her back. He hadn't asked to come in and he hadn't asked for her number; they'd just said their goodnights and he'd staggered off down the street.

"Is anybody there? Gail?" She blinked. Tom loomed over her desk; she forced a smile. "How are you feeling?"

"Bit better." She felt herself stiffen.

"We put a fair bit away, didn't we?"

"We didn't half." There was an awkward pause.

Tom nodded. "You okay for coffee?"

Gail thought of Rob again: their lazy Sunday mornings. ("For coffee? F'coffee." Throwing a V-sign: "F'coff.") "Yes, thanks. Still got my two o'clock brew." She grabbed her mouse and started blindly scanning her monitor. Another pause.

"Are you okay?"

"Yeah, I'm fine. Just tired." She was hoping he'd go away.

"Right. I'm glad you came round last night."

"Me too." This time the smile felt genuine even though she had a blinking fit as she said it. She felt him looking at her.

"I'll let you get on, then."

She watched Tom's rear elevation slink off towards the kitchen then went back to scanning her monitor. Soon her eyes defocused again.

"I never got your number!" she'd called out in the minimarket near her house. She'd found him staring at the baked beans. He'd turned around and dropped a tin he was balancing on a loaf of bread, which in turn was perched on top of a can of soup. Straight away, she regretted saying anything to him, conscious of what she might look like under cold, sober lights. She remembered flushing and both of them going for the tin. He got there first and she looked down at him. His hair was tied back and he had on a snug, red tee shirt and dark brown cords.

"Hello," he said.

"Hiya, Robert."

"Robert? Only my mum calls me Robert. How's it going?"

"You need a basket. Use mine if you like. I never got your number."

"Thanks. I don't have one." He started putting his shopping in her basket. "Well, I tell a lie, I do but it's knackered. The phone. What's your number?"

Her stomach had fluttered but she hadn't felt herself blushing again. It had felt so natural. So inevitable.

There was a loud, deep clang outside in the building site. She jumped and looked up, then tried to carry on with her work.

## 5

The drove road felt ancient and unused but he had a niggling feeling, like he'd left the house without taking something important with him. He'd remembered to douse his campfire and cover it with earth and pine needles, so that wasn't it. The track climbed among three looming rocky peaks, curling round to the east as it followed the water of three small lochs, black and forgotten. Here the mountains seemed to lean in on him, watching him. Or protecting him.

After yesterday's ordeal he'd considered travelling at night, but thought better of it now. Navigating in the dark would be difficult and sleeping during the day would be dangerous. "No, better to stick to the plan." Ten or twelve miles a day until he got to Thurso. "Then I'll be safe." He could do more, but had to ration his strength. He wasn't eating much and after seven or eight miles per day he was starting to feel shaky and light-headed.

The third loch was more of a pond. Still and lifeless. The track curved round to the left at the foot of the mountain. Here the loch drained into a wide, shallow burn. It prattled to him above the hoarse whisper of the wind. He was about to open the map when he looked up and saw a pack of black dogs just round the bend. He almost fell over trying to stop, and pain from his ankle shot up his leg. They looked like wolves or wolfhounds: large with sharp faces. All sitting or lying down, waiting. He could see their eyes. He hunched and slowly moved towards the mountain.

The land to the east was open moorland dotted with large plantations. The map showed that it was flat all the way to Thurso. He swore at himself for not seeing this route before.

Most of the dogs were lying down now. "Who sent you?" He side-stepped off the track towards the gurgling burn. "Are you working alone?" He tried to keep the dogs in sight while glancing down at the green rocks as he forded the stream, planting each foot as surely as he could. The dogs hadn't seen him, or they weren't interested in him. Maybe they were sent just to intimidate him. "Maybe they're all chained up over there."

The land was boggy again beyond the burn and it rose up to a low plateau. The dogs became dots at the foot of the mountain. He felt a small surge of triumph. But he would have to be wary of new threats. "They're definitely watching the roads now."

## 6

The hotel bar was how he liked it: dark, low ceiling, thick carpets, dark-stained half-panelled walls, elsewhere painted bottle green, nooks and crannies, alcoves and booths, horse brasses and stained-glass partitions with scenes of fox and grouse hunting. Some Scottish folk music was playing very quietly somewhere above his head. Behind the bar, the young Australian woman in the tight tartan leggings eyed Rob with disdain as he sat sipping the pint she'd served him. Soldier's Leap, it was called. Hoppy and refreshing.

A few customers were having a late lunch. Across the room sat a couple about his age and their young twins with long, almost white, blonde hair. A chocolate Labrador sat like a sphinx, panting under their table. The mother didn't so much chastise the children as showcase their misbehaviour. She spoke loud Estuary English while one of the twins stood on a chair, bashing her empty plastic bottle on the table top.

"Fern," she sang. "What are you doing?" Fern ignored her. The other twin was trying to draw the curtains behind her father, who sat reading a leaflet. "Barnie, look out for Bracken."

Rob spat a mouthful of beer. "Fern and Bracken," he said, too loudly. "Priceless."

"Fern, are you being naughty?" The mother looked around at Bracken again, who had drawn one curtain and was working on the other. "Barnie."

"What?"

"Bracken."

Barnie looked round at his daughter. "What? She's all right."

Fern was still pounding the bottle on the table. "Come on now, Fern. You've had your fun." Again, the girl ignored her.

Rob finished his pint and stood up noisily, steadying himself on the sides of the alcove. As he zigzagged past the mother he caught her eye and stopped. "Bracken is highly poisonous, you know."

"Sorry?"

"Bracken is poisonous." The mother looked at him

with an expression that feigned incomprehension. Rob glanced at her lips; they looked soft and supple but her mouth was a bit too big. Then he looked at Barnie, who was still oblivious to this life he'd chosen. Rob placed his glass on a beer towel at the bar and worked his way upstairs to his room. He thought he might have a wank over the mother later.

## 7

The forest loomed up. The land was open and he felt exposed. The sun shone through rain that fell in slow motion. Low barking sounds behind him. He spun around to see a group of nine or ten Watchers leading black hounds towards him. The Watchers took long strides that didn't look right, like they were skating across the ground. He turned and ran, his legs feeling heavy, his ankle still smarting. The forest seemed miles away. This time he wouldn't look back. He had to reach the trees. He had to get to Thurso.

He dismissed a stupid thought about shedding his pack. The barking was louder now. The trees drew closer. He could beat them. His injured foot found a divot and he squealed as the pain shot into his brain like a bolt. He tumbled over the heath, grimacing, retching in pain and anguish. He pulled himself to his feet, crying out. The ankle already felt stiff and swollen. "Don't look back." The trees were closer but so was the barking. These were their best men: he must've done something terrible. He ran two steps on his good foot to every one on his injured one.

Grunting or crying out each time. The eaves of the forest were almost within reach. The barking was right behind him; he could hear the Watchers' breathing.

As he passed the first trees he heard the hounds snarl, could feel their teeth at his heels. He ran through the trees and found quiet. He sucked in cool pine air, smiling, laughing, rubbing his scalp. "These are their best men?" Maybe they were. But they'd be angry now. They'd send reinforcements. A small swarm of cleg-birds bothered him for a few seconds until he wafted them away. "At least you don't bite."

## 8

After a dinner of haggis, tatties and neeps, which he could hardly taste and would later forget, Rob sat in a large, shiny, wing chair in the Robertson Arms, intent on drinking himself silly. He'd already started working his way through the beers for the second time, from left to right along the bar. He was halfway through when the group of golfers came in.

"Brian!" Rob shouted, and Brian and a few of the others turned. Rob threw up his hand in greeting and they turned towards the bar, muttering and puzzled. Rob placed a beer mat on top of his pint and tottered over towards the golfers. He filled a gap at the bar and turned to one of the younger men. "Addagoodroundlads?"

"Yeah, mate. Not bad."

"Youknowwhattheysayboutgoff. Golf. Donya?

Eh?"

"What's that mate?"

"Sagoodwalkspoil."

One of the older men said: "Really? I've never heard that before." And the golfers laughed.

Rob sought out Brian. "Where's, wheresBrian?" He squinted at the younger man. "Whasyourname?"

"Graham."

"Graham. Goodname Graham. Whereyoufrom?"

"Well, I'm from Surrey and this lot are from Yorkshire."

"Yorkshire. Myneckowoods. Wherebouts inYorksh?"

Brian took a step forward with his pint. Rob looked down at huge, work-worn hands and then up at lips the colour of raw liver. "Doncaster."

"Doncaster! Doncaster's worsmistake Romans evmade. AfterCasford Castlefordocourse."

Some of the golfers laughed; Brian didn't. "Why? What's wrong with Doncaster?" He spoke as if his mouth was full of cotton wool.

"Sashitole. Imean. What is the point oDoncaster?"

"Well I like it. And so does he, and so does he."

"YouknowDoncaster's AIDScapalofEnglan? Eh? AvyougotAIDS Bri?"

Brian planted his large, calloused fist into the middle of Rob's face. He felt a shock of pain radiate from his nose like an electrical current and then the worst headache he'd ever had. He slumped to his knees, hanging onto the brass bar and rocking his head with slurred laughter.

"There. You little twat." Brian's friends were

holding him back and whoaing him like he was a shire horse. Rob was hearing advice not to hit him again and suggestions to leave the pub. Rob climbed up the front of the bar. The blood from his nose looked like a messy goatee beard. He looked around for Brian and threw a wild punch. He caught the older man on the ear; someone else pushed him and another punched him in the stomach. He crumpled up and the golfers' voices faded out and then blackness. He came round to a local accent asking him if he was all right. He saw a lime-green blur, realised it was a police officer.

"Anyoucanfuckoffanall!"

## 9

David found a couple of good trees deep within the forest and stretched his tarp between them. He'd watched the moon laughing as he ate his trout and savoury rice, and he'd laughed back. But now a thin layer of cloud provided a fine rain that sizzled on the fabric above him, relaxing him. His eyes adjusted to the oily dark. He could see the nearer tree trunks like columns in a burnt-out church but that was all. The rest of the world had stopped existing. The trees were whispering and taunting but he'd heard it all before. He kept reminding himself that as long as they were hiding him, they were his friends. "Just not very supportive ones."

It was the Watchers he had to worry about now. He felt the damp cold in his bones but he was assured he wouldn't be attracting any unwanted attention:

he'd decided to douse his fire before he settled down for the night.

He remembered the dream again.

It was soon after David had put Sheldon in the hospital that he'd been sent to Inverness. The Shearwater Psychiatric Unit. That's why they ended up moving there. It didn't seem to do much good. He still had the night terrors, the dreams. He was in there for the best part of a year and they tried all sorts of different medications – lithium, olanzapine, clozapine, lurasidone – but most of them made him feel like shite. In the end, they put him on a combination of quetiapine and venlafaxine, and discharged him.

He took his magic sweeties all through college and he earned three A-levels: English, Maths and History. After college he had a succession of no-hoper jobs. None lasted more than a couple of years, mainly due to boredom rather than the side-effects. These were the happy years. He'd go out with the lads from college at the weekends. Matt and Joe would get motherless while he drank his lime and soda and they'd all end up at The Crypt on Union Street. David would jump around like an epileptic to whichever band they'd brought up from Edinburgh or Glasgow then he'd watch as the others tried to pull girls.

He left his twenties behind and started to yearn for something more meaningful than the endless cycle of what had come before. It was at this time that he saw an advert in *The Herald* for positions at the Scottish Ambulance Service. They needed call-takers. Here was something worth doing. Something where he could make a difference – to give something back.

He prepared for the interview and had a good idea of the questions he would be asked. A blonde team leader called Cheryl and a nice wee redhead from HR interviewed him. He'd learned all the facts about the organization and reeled them off when prompted. He smiled a lot and sat upright, maintained eye contact, but just enough so he didn't look weird. Confident but not cocky. Within the first three minutes he knew he had the job: the interviewers smiled and nodded at his answers. Cheryl phoned him later in the day and said they'd been really impressed. He'd been there ever since, making a difference, giving something back.

Now he nestled his hooded head into a soft depression in his pack. He took a glove off and felt for the compass in his coat pocket. It wasn't there. He felt right into the corners but it wasn't there. He sat tight upright and padded all his coat pockets, clambered to his knees and rubbed his hips and thighs. It wasn't there. "No," he breathed. "I just had it." He stared about the camp, wishing that he had a torch. "I just fucking had it."

"Keep your voice down," a tree whispered.

"I just had it, though." He felt about him through the dry earth and pine needles under the tarp, trying to think when he'd last touched the compass. "Where are you?" He could feel himself wanting to cry and tried to control his panic with deep breaths. "Where are you? Eh?" His breathing was getting faster and he felt the sting of tears. "Where are you?" he gurgled and dropped to his hip.

"Keep quiet," the trees said.

He wrapped an arm around his head and the sobs

shuddered through him. "Where are you?" He shifted his weight and stretched his legs out and felt something digging into the back of his knee. He knew it was the compass before he slid his hand down into the sleeping bag. He brought it out. He thumbed the lid and tightened his fist around it, then slipped it into his coat pocket and zipped it in.

## 10

"Wake up."

A memory or a dream: the dual carriageway coming out of Inverness. The back seat of Dad's car, behind Mum. Dad driving. Ali was resting the back of his head against the back window ledge. He felt the soothing cold of the metal on his temple. He watched the orange lights gliding past. He tried to follow them but it made him dizzy so he looked through them and let his vision blur.

They'd stopped at Nairn at a place Dad knew called Chish and Fips. Dad drove down to the quayside and they'd stared across Moray Firth towards the Black Isle and the hills beyond. Ali blew on his chips and watched mauve cumulus clouds rushing beneath a canvas of cirrocumulus. How they looked like they had been put there. The car was full of laughter and the smell of vinegar. He remembered laughing along, not sure why.

And then the passing lights, pulsing in the darkness.

He awoke in his bed to the sound of Mum

downstairs, shouting and crying. Ali could barely hear Dad's voice and that made him all the more terrifying. Mum became quiet for a moment, then she yelped like a kicked dog. Then she was quiet again. Then screaming, begging, pleading, things being broken. And, all the time, Dad was silent.

Ali woke later and heard footsteps on the stairs; the creak of the tenth step. His heart pounded and he tightened his eyes shut. Dad had never hit him before. Maybe this time he was really angry. Ali sensed the light from the landing through his eyelids, heard Mum's snuffling, like she had a cold. She didn't turn the bedroom light on.

"Wake up."

He felt her hand on his shoulder. The gentlest of touches. He thought about pretending to sleep until she went away.

"Wake up, Ali-bear."

But he knew he couldn't. He opened his eyes and Mum's silhouette was next to him. He felt her soft, dry hand on his forehead and cheek.

"What's wrong, Mummy?"

"Nothing, love. Me and Daddy have just had a wee argument. That's all."

She was kneeling next to his bed, her yellow hair glowing in the soft light from the landing. He could see her eye, already swollen, starting to turn dark. And the tears and the smeared make-up. And the red marks on her neck. Frank Sinatra was singing downstairs.

Ali propped himself up on his elbow and Mum wrapped her arms around him and pulled him to her. He hung his arms over her shoulders and smelled her perfume and she juddered and sobbed. Ali felt his own tears rising from his throat and he buried his face into Mum's hair.

"I love you, Ali." She pushed him forward so she could look at his face. "You know that, don't you?"

And he'd nodded through his tears. Mum had held him like that until he'd fallen asleep.

"Wake up."

## 11

The custody suite in Pitlochry Police Station consisted of one room. It reminded Rob of one of the meeting rooms at work, except there was a bed in it. There was a camera hidden in a black, plastic ball in one corner of the ceiling. He threw a couple of fingers at it intermittently, accompanied by mumbled swearing and weak laughter. He pressed his nose until it started to hurt. It had stopped bleeding but he still dabbed his nostrils with the back of his hand.

"Ahjuswanyour. Exratimenyour. D-l-l-l-l-l. Kiss." It couldn't be called singing. He wanted to talk to Gail but they'd taken his phone. "Wheresmephone? Wanmephone!" He sat up and swung his legs over the side of the bed, nearly toppling over. He moaned and leaned forward, planted his elbows on his knees. He interlocked his fingers and twisted his wedding ring.

"Fuck it." He stood up and zigzagged over to the door, slapped on it. "Hello? Hello? Need to make aphonecall." Now he thumped the door. "Hello? Hello!"

He continued thumping until a woman's voice on the other side said: "Step away from the door." He did so and a few seconds later she unlocked the door, swung it wide and stepped forward. Rob pretended he wasn't drunk. "Hello." He tilted his head to one side. "I wonder if you'd be so kind as to let me make a phone call." Down the hall a radio was trickling Neil Diamond.

"You don't have the right to a phone call."

"What if I needed a sol, slistor?"

"Are you going to behave and sleep it off?"

"I needto talk tomy wife. She doesn't know where I am."

The policewoman puffed. She had a kind, round face and shiny, dark hair. "If you behave yourself, I'll let you phone her. Just to check in. Then it's off to bed. And quiet. Is that a deal?"

"Yes sir, ma'am, madam." His head dropped and he gave a little salute. He looked up at her lips: he'd made her smile.

He followed her down the hall towards the entrance. The desk sergeant straightened up from his Sudoku and glanced at him. The policewoman twisted the phone round and offered Rob the receiver. He stepped forward and dialled the landline. He looked at the clock. Good – it was only half past eleven. The phone rang for a long time and then he remembered the phone was downstairs and she was probably upstairs.

"Hello?" She sounded as if he'd woken her up.

He cleared his throat. "Hello. Gail. It's me."

A pause, then quiet and fragile: "Where are you?"

"Scoland."

"Well I guessed that. Whereabouts? Why have you been ignoring my texts? I've been worried sick. Just leaving me like that without any explanation. Why can't you just talk to me? I've had to lie to Steve and—"

He hung up and grinned at the desk sergeant. "Juswanted to hear her voice."

"Okay. Do you want to get some shut-eye now?"

"Yes, sir. If you'll be so kind as to have someone

escort me to my room." The policewoman touched his upper arm and he followed her back to his cell. He turned to her as they walked. "What's your name, then?" he grinned.

"I thought you were going to behave."


## 12


Ali listened to the birds through his open window. It was still muggy and he lay on top of his bed covers in nothing but his shorts. His hand had stopped throbbing but he still couldn't move his fingers. The bruise would be gone before school, though. He stared at the ceiling and thought about the dream.

He must've been about five or six. It was just before Mum went away, anyway. She was talking to Auntie Fiona in the kitchen. Dad was at work. Ali was playing with his cars in the hallway. He could hear them almost whispering. He thought Mum was crying. After a while, Mum came into the hall and picked him up. Her eyes looked sore. She said that no matter what happened next, she loved him.

The day after that she was gone. Dad didn't talk about it at first but when he got older and naughtier he would tell him off and say that Mum had left because of him, because he was naughty and she couldn't handle it.

Maybe she was dead now, like Dad said.

But Auntie Fiona was still alive. He'd try the bus plan again. After he'd thought it through more carefully. Dad would have to look after himself now.

There was a soft knock at the door and then the key turned. Ali looked up to see Dad's head there. He came into the room and sat on the end of his bed. Ali slid his feet up, away from him.

"How's your hand?"

Ali's voice was brittle: "It's all right, Father."

"Good. Good. You know I love you, don't you?"

"Aye, Father."

Dad touched his foot, stroked it. Then he stood up and undid his belt. "But you need to be disciplined." He was almost whispering. Ali stared at Dad's hands as they undid his fly. "On your knees, boy."

"Father, no."

"What do you mean, no?" That paper and comb voice. "Do you think you get to call the shots? After all you've done?" He wrapped his belt around his knuckles. "It's either one or the other, boy. One or the other." Ali curled up against his head-board, staring at the skirting-board near the door. "Do I have to tell you again?"

Ali unwound and turned onto his belly, slid his arms underneath himself. He buried his face into the pillow. He felt Dad climbing onto the bed behind him. Dad yanked his shorts down and then gently worked them over his ankles and feet. Ali sank and rolled as Dad hung over him. He felt soft hands on his knees as Dad pulled his legs apart, then the arms planted on the bed against Ali's shoulders. His breath smelled of whisky. He tried to shrink away from his touch but he couldn't.

Then splitting pain. He whimpered. He heard Dad moan. He felt tears stinging his eyes. Dad lifted him off the bed onto his knees and then his hands were clammy, clamped around his waist. The movement got quicker and Ali yelped in pain. Now he was sobbing and he heard Dad saying "Shh". Soon, Dad jerked and his hold around his ribs tightened. He moaned again, louder than before. He could hear him sucking air through his teeth. The relief from the pain was like warm water flooding over him. Ali dropped back onto the bed and screwed himself up, crying into his arm. He heard Dad's heavy breathing and his zip and his belt buckle.

"Go and have a shower." Then the door was opened then closed and he was alone again.

# THURSDAY

## 1

Rob took the road out of town, onto a dual carriageway, ever northward. He had a thick head and a mouldy tongue. He couldn't face any noise so he listened to the music of the engine instead. The sun dashed between low, restless clouds, their shadows sliding across the green land.

He put Fern and Bracken's mum out of his mind with memories of Gail. They didn't have sex that first night even though he wanted to. He supposed he wasn't as assertive back then. But it made it all the better when they did have sex for the first time.

He remembered being caught off guard when she found him in the mini-market on Granville Road. It was a bit awkward because he was sober. He'd asked for her phone number and had felt a strange elation he'd not felt with other girls he'd met. They strolled along the streets of Fallowfield for nearly two hours, talking, joking, laughing. He carried her shopping and the bag handles dug into his fingers but he didn't care. She brought out a silly, child-like side in him that he didn't know he had.

They arranged to go to her local. Their first date consisted of drinking a lot and laughing, mainly at the expense of the pub's other patrons. He went to the bar while she went to the toilet and they both got back to their table together. He put their drinks down and she'd kissed him again before they sat down.

That's what he missed most: her vitality and spontaneity. They rushed their pints and went back to her house in Whalley Range, stopping now and then for juicy kisses in darkened doorways. From that night until the middle of – when? 2005? – they'd had sex nearly every day. Except when she'd abandoned him in Manchester after her graduation.

Now the road sped up the wide valley of Glen Garry to the Drumochter Summit. Here the land was high, flat and bleak. Little orange packs of workmen went about their inscrutable business at the edge of the road and along little tracks up the side of the valley.

At Dalwhinnie, he turned left and drove into mist and cloud towards Loch Laggan. He came to a wide beach and thought that he'd come to an inlet of the sea. As he made his way along the shore, he saw a small Fiat parked at a funny angle on the grass verge.

"Dogging," he muttered. Soon after, a couple were walking down the road away from him. The woman turned and gave him the international sign for phone. He sped on.

"Please turn around when possible," Diane said.

"Fuck 'em," he replied.

"It is – eighteen miles – to the next garage."

"Shut up, bitch." He drove into Spean Bridge and found the nearest hotel.

## 2

The capsules were easy enough to empty. He just had to twist the two halves and ease them apart. He poured the powder into a jam jar.

It was getting the pills in the first place that was difficult. Dad kept his amitriptyline in the sideboard drawer near his stereo. "Three Coins in a Fountain" was playing. Ali wanted to turn it off but he knew it would wake him. He sat in his Big Chair with his head to one side, slavering.

He knew the drawer was noisy. It didn't have any runners and the wood might stick when he pulled it. He lifted the drawer as he eased it out, looking at Dad all the while. It cracked and Dad started and cleared his throat. Ali froze. Dad's head rolled over to the other side. The drawer was open about three inches. He removed things and tried to remember where they'd been. The bottle was underneath Dad's wallet. He kept glancing at Dad, listening, as he slid the bottle out and pocketed it. Then he replaced the other things in the order he'd removed them.

The drawer slid shut and he crept towards the door in his bare feet.

In the kitchen he knifed the tuna out of the tin into a bowl, cut it up and sprinkled the amitriptyline over the top. He squirted more salad cream into the bowl than usual and mixed it all until it was smooth and the powder was invisible. He experimented with flour, salt and sugar but none of them were right. The capsules just didn't weigh the same as the ones with the drug in. In the end he mixed flour and salt together, made a little funnel out of paper and tipped a small amount into each empty capsule. He reassembled each capsule, wiped them off and put them carefully back into the bottle.

## 3

Another town, another pub. The Loch Loyne in Spean Bridge was a tall, handsome Georgian building, squeezed between a gift shop and a chemist. Rob parked up at the rear and took his overnight bag into the bar.

He heard piped folk music while he ate fish and chips with a couple of pints of amber, floral beer called Redemption.

After, he went to his room and lay on his bed, hoping to cure his hangover with some sleep. One of the springs was digging into his back, even through the duvet. An annoying shaft of afternoon sunlight warmed his face and coloured the backs of his eyelids.

The room smelled of Turkish delight. He rolled off the bed and went to draw the curtains when his phone rang. He picked it up and thought about ignoring it.

"Hello."

"Hi. It's me."

"Hello, you."

"What happened last night?"

"I was a bit drunk. I was missing you."

"It was nice of you to phone."

He didn't know if she was being sarcastic or not. "Mmm. What have you been up to?"

"Not much. Working. Went out for a curry with Tom."

"Did you?"

"Yes."

"Just like that?"

"Well, you abandoned me. So I took up a friend's offer of company."

"He's your friend, is he?"

"You know we're friends."

"Just Good Friends."

"He's been very kind to me over the past few days."

"I bet he has. What else you been doing with him?"

"I went round to his for dinner and he looked after me."

"He looked after you? You know what? Just fuck off."

He hung up.

## 4

Gail sniffed and thought of Tom. His carved lips, his angular shoulders. She picked up the large glass of red wine by the stem and twisted off her dining chair. A dish of half-eaten spaghetti Bolognese and the crumbs of a fully eaten garlic bread on the smoked glass dining table.

She sat on the over-sized sofa and picked up her mechanical pencil and clipboard with plain white A4. Drawing soothed her. She supposed it took her back to a happier time.

Soon after she'd graduated, Gail had moved back to Newcastle to be closer to her parents, something that Rob didn't understand. And he'd sulked like a spoilt child when she told him. He didn't speak to her for three days. Rob stayed on at Vinyl Countdown, the shop he'd been working at since his own graduation, but after a few months he moved back to Leeds.

They kept in touch. He wrote letters to her with little poems and drawings on them; she still had them in a shoe box somewhere. They'd seen each other most weekends and the sex had been all the more intense.

Tonight was warm and clear and someone nearby was playing Take That's Greatest Hits louder than was acceptable on her street. She didn't mind tonight. She didn't give a fuck tonight. She sang along now and then as she drew, almost muttering the words. Tears pinked her eyes and she dabbed them with a soggy tissue.

Gail sometimes wished she was still in the flat in

the city centre. Before they stopped having fun. She'd got what she wanted, mainly against Rob's wishes: they'd bought a house – an actual house with more than three rooms – and moved out of the flat eight years ago. Now she looked around their nice big living room with its deep, dark chocolate carpets and shiny leather furniture and it felt cold and empty.

The bastard had hung up on her. And when she'd tried to phone his mobile it was switched off again.

At least he was alive.

She put the clipboard and her pencil on the arm of the sofa. Tom's lips and his eyes. His square pecs. His washboard stomach. She hadn't had sex in five years. She slid down and sank into the sofa, pulled her skirt past her hips.

Rob had, though.

She spread her legs and slid her hand under the top of her pants. His large, soft hands on her arse, making gentle circles. She ran her middle finger along her lips, parted them. She was already wet. His firm lips on hers, his hot tongue in her mouth. The taste of him. She put her finger inside then brought it wet to her clitoris, making slow little circles. His huge cock sliding into her. Her hands on his thighs, easing him inside.

It didn't take her long to come. It never did.

## 5

Fraser couldn't prove anything. But he knew when the boy was telling the truth and when he was lying. His pills were intact. The bottle was underneath his wallet in the drawer where he'd left them. He held the bottle up to the light and counted them, judged the weight of the bottle. He made a fist around the pills and stared through the rain at the gathering dusk. Something was off. The sandwich didn't taste right. There was no doubt. It wasn't unpleasant; it just wasn't right. So he'd thrown it away and made himself a ham sandwich.

He would have to visit the boy again, question him further, discipline him. If it took the rest of the year, he would show him right from wrong and who was Boss. Sure enough, the boy didn't find it at all pleasant but that was the point, wasn't it? He would visit the boy tonight and every night until he learned some respect.

## 6

Rob had a long sleep and a refreshing shower. He popped another two paracetamol and took his time getting dressed. After an early dinner he started on the beer. There were only three ales; he preferred the Redemption, and stuck with that for the rest of the night.

The pub was larger than it looked from the street. It went back for yards, and a narrow side corridor linked many small, dark rooms, made cosy with the orange glow of gaslight. The corridor led finally down a few steps to a larger bar room and the beer garden. The bar had steadily been filling up since dinner; at about eight, a group of men came in with instrument cases.

"Oh, God," Rob moaned. He watched them set up, which meant moving a table out of the way and stacking their empty cases in a corner. There was a guitar, violin, accordion and what might have been a mandolin but he wasn't sure. He was surprised to see that only two of the musicians had beards.

They started tuning up and the tables and chairs around them filled. A group of four came to the table next to his. Three women and a man who looked gay. One of the women glanced at him as she sat down furthest away from him. She smiled and he gave her one back: his best pulling smile. He wasn't usually one for smiling unless he meant it but he'd learned to fake it over the years. It was all about the eyes.

She wasn't bad-looking. A few years younger than he was, maybe. Black eyes, slightly too far apart, her dark hair parted in the middle and tucked behind her ears. She was pretty, even though she wasn't putting much effort into it. He liked that. He checked the other two. Both blonde, pretty much interchangeable. Number One's fringe twitched when she blinked. She wasn't as good-looking as the brunette. Number Two was better but she hadn't given him the eye.

He felt the brunette looking at him again and he held her for a second or two, smiling, until she looked away. Under the table, he turned his wedding ring with his left thumb.

The band started up with a song that sounded familiar. Everyone else seemed to know it intimately and most sang along on the chorus. They played a fast jig after that and everyone slapped their knees in time. Rob even found himself tapping his foot and started drinking his pint quicker. Halfway through the third song he went to the bar and smelled the log fire burning. That was the reason it was so warm. It had turned cooler today, but not cold enough for a fire. He took his pint back to the table and glanced at the brunette again. Slowly, slowly, catchy monkey.

Soon a grey haze started to form at the ceiling. It became thicker as the band played some ballad or other, but no one seemed to mind. When the haze had reached halfway to the floor, people started coughing and he heard an old woman say: "Is something burning?" A moment later, one of the barmen strode into the middle of the crowd and announced that the chimney was blocked. The band did not falter. They played the last few bars of their song and made their way outside with everyone else, holding their instruments under their arms, laughing and shouting.

Rob looked around for her in the damp beer garden. Her friends were hunched over their drinks, huddling together with their hoods up. He saw her off to the side, hugging herself and smoking a roll up. He pocketed his wedding ring, sauntered over.

"How's it going?" he said.

"Hello."

"Enjoying the music?"

"Aye. Yourself?"

"It's not bad. Don't really go for folk. It's good fun, though. What's your name?"

"Abi."

"Abi. Abigail."

"Aye." She smiled and took a drag. He stared at the small mouth wrapped tight around the roll-up.

"Kirk Hammerton, bon viveur." He held out his hand.

"Your full name? Good to know." She coughed and took his hand. "Isn't Kirk Hammerton a village in Yorkshire?" She had a little ski-jump nose that twitched when she said certain words.

"Er, you got me there."

"Are you from Yorkshire?"

"Used to be. How come you've heard of Kirk Hammerton?"

"I've been there, I think, or I drove through it once. I might've seen it on a map."

He looked at her friends and saw the man looking back with a smile. "Who you with?" he said, nodding at them.

She pointed them out: "That's Iain, Jules and Vicky."

"Where are you from?"

"Edinburgh."

"Lovely place. Beautiful. You on holiday?"

"Aye. Just for the week. Back to work on Monday. What are you up to?"

"Just driving around, seeing the sights." He nodded and she nodded back. She stared at the end of her roll-up when she took a drag.

The landlord appeared at the door. "Okay, folks.

Disaster has been averted."

Someone said: "What was it, John?"

"A balloon, of all things. Must've found its way up there after Neil's fiftieth."

Some people cheered and laughed and the beer garden started to empty. The band started playing as they made their way back inside. Rob looked back at Abi. She was perhaps an inch taller than him. She smiled down at him.

"Where have you come from today?" she tried.

"Er, Pitlochry?"

"Oh aye. Did you see the distillery?"

"Yeh. Interesting is not the word."

"Do you like whisky?"

"It's –"

"I love whisky. I've got a fifteen year old in my room."

"Isn't that illegal?" She stared at him for a moment then laughed, a protracted near-scream punctuated with little snorts that made her laugh even more. "Eh?" Rob said.

"Whisky, silly," she said, touching his arm. "Would you come up for a wee dram?"

"Er, yeah, okay, then."

They had sex three different ways and he made her come, so it was a good night. Afterwards they lay back, the duvet piled up near the door. It was even warmer up here than in the bar. He tried to avoid the annoying bed spring. She didn't seem to mind his paunch and she even stroked it while she nestled her head in the crook of his arm. She had a great body: wide hips and small, pert breasts. Her skin was pale and had the odd little mole.

"You're a big laddie, aren't you? For a wee laddie." She cupped his balls and gave them the gentlest of squeezes, then swung her legs over the side of the bed.

"I'm… blessed. Thank you." He laughed.

She poured more whisky into her plastic cup. "Another?"

He glanced at his cup but knew it was still almost full. "I'm okay, thanks."

She looked over her shoulder at him and her hair hid one of her eyes. "What are you running from, Kirk Hammerton?"

"Running? I'm not running from anything."

"You have a wife. I can see the mark on your finger."

He looked at his hand and puffed. "You got me again."

"Everything happens for a reason, Kirk."

"Does it fuck. Where did that come from?" He laughed again. "You think there's some kind of meaning to all this? To life?"

"Of course there is, Kirk –"

"Listen. There aren't many people in the history of the world who've made an actual difference. Maybe your composers, your artists, architects, scientists. They're the people who ever mattered. The rest of us are just killing time."

"You can't really—"

"I'll tell you the meaning of life. Life is just a load of chemical reactions and electrical impulses. We're born alone and we die alone and we all try to scrape together as much happiness as we can in between."

"I'm sorry you feel that way."

So was Rob sometimes. He didn't say anything else. He wasn't about to get into some Mickey Mouse philosophical discussion with some bird he'd just shagged.

He stood and inched open the curtains. He found the moon, high and out of focus. He necked his whisky.

Maybe they weren't meant to be together. They'd had a good run and it was time to move on. Was it worth fighting for? Maybe he was meant to be alone. Maybe there wasn't anyone out there for him. There were only so many women in the world.

In another universe, he could've fallen for Abi from Edinburgh.


# 7


The rain kept coming. Ali lay on his side, sobbing silently. His pillow was wet and sticky with tears and snot but he didn't care. He dabbed his bum with a ball of toilet paper. He lifted himself from the bed and pulled his arm across his nose.

As well as locking the door, Dad had nailed the window shut. He'd have to find another way out. Ali opened his wardrobe and started putting some clothes into his school bag. He'd need money and some food for the journey but he'd worry about that later. His bike was in the shed so he would need the key from Dad's key ring. He'd take the bike down the cliff path and sleep in the den.

A couple of weeks ago, someone had dumped a mattress near the docks and it had taken all morning to lug it up the hill and across the field to the cliff path. No one knew about the den. Not Dad. Not PC Gary. Not Miss Palmer. He would be safe there until morning. The den would be comfortable and dry but it might be cold. He pulled his winter coat from his divan drawer and laid it on top of his school bag at the bottom of the wardrobe.

## 8

When she was about seven, Gail's teacher, Miss Barrett, asked the class what they wanted to be when they grew up. The boys said they wanted to be train drivers and footballers and the girls wanted to be dancers and nurses. Gail said she wanted to design bridges, and everyone, including Miss Barrett, laughed at her.

She played with Lego a lot at that time but she found she wasn't able to build bridges with long spans like she wanted to. On her eighth birthday, her dad gave her a Meccano set and that was when her interest became an obsession. Every bit of pocket money went towards new pieces; she asked for new Meccano for Christmas and birthdays. Within a few years she was able to build an exact structural copy of the Forth Rail Bridge.

She asked Dad all sorts of questions about bridges but he didn't know the answers. She could remember losing one of her books and, after a long search, finding it among Dad's work things. He said he borrowed it and had been reading it during his breaks.

At school, she excelled at Maths and Science. During French and History lessons she doodled bridges of all kinds: suspension, cable-stayed, arched, bowstring, cantilevered, swing bridges. For an art assignment she drew, in meticulous detail, the Pont de Saint-Bénezet in Avignon: the chapel, the four surviving wide arches, the cutwaters.

The obsession lasted until she was about thirteen, when she learned about clothes and music and boys. But she'd never lost her interest in bridges. She'd studied Maths and Physics at A-level and had gone on to study Civil Engineering at university.

Now she straightened her pants and pulled her skirt back down. She picked up the clip board and pencil and continued with her drawing. The Tyne Bridge. She knew it by heart now. The beautiful curve, the exact number of trusses. She put the ball of her thumb to her forehead and tears poured and spattered onto the clipboard. She dropped the pencil and put both hands over her eyes and sat there for a long time.

Then she rose and climbed the stairs up to the bathroom and took the little packet out of the medicine cabinet and sat on the edge of the bath. She pulled her skirt to her lap and took a razor blade from the little packet and she made a neat little cut across the top of her left thigh. She was careful to make it parallel and the same length as the older ones. Blood trickled down the sides of her thigh and she made another cut. Parallel, same length. She watched her tears dripping onto her thigh, mixing with the blood that was now trickling onto the floor. Then she threw the razor blade into the sink.

She laughed through her tears: she was glad the floor tiles were dark grey.

## 9

Sheldon showed him the blue, floppy baby. Grinning Sheldon.

"I hope you're happy."

David wasn't sure if it was Sheldon or the trees.

He'd come home from work and gone straight to the fridge for a beer. There was half of the apple crumble Mum had brought round. He'd taken the tin foil off and screwed it up and taken a dessert spoon from the draining board. He leaned against the worktop and stuffed big spoonfuls of crumble into his mouth, washed it down with glugs of beer. He didn't usually drink after a night shift but he'd had two children choking, one after the other. On the second call, the woman was trying to listen to his instructions but the man just wouldn't shut up. It was 4.30 in the morning on his fourth night on the trot and he'd lost his rag. Carolyn, his team leader, had had to take him to one side after the call.

He knew the beer would knock him out. He felt floaty as he started on the second half of the bottle. The pale dawn half-lit the kitchen. The neighbour's baby was crying again. Maybe he wouldn't get straight off to sleep after all. It wasn't the baby that got to him but the mother. She just wouldn't or couldn't shut the baby up. She was Polish or Lithuanian. Vanya, she was called. He'd said hello to her a couple of times when she'd been hanging the washing out. She had a husband but he never seemed to be there.

He climbed the stairs and dumped his uniform on the floor next to the wash basket. His mum would wash it tomorrow or Monday. His bed was cool, soft, welcoming. The baby's wailing had followed him upstairs. Their bedroom was next to his. The baby seemed to be in pain and Vanya had just shouted at it, probably telling it to stop, screaming, swearing. The baby seemed to be next to the wall. David put a pillow over his exposed ear but the muffling just seemed to isolate the noise. The baby screamed and then started crying even louder. Vanya repeated the same word over and over but the baby wasn't listening.

David found himself downstairs in the front room in nothing but his shorts. He heard the baby's screaming just as loud as in the bedroom. He put the ball of his thumb to his temple, tightened his eyes. His hand was gripping the front door handle. He turned the key and then he was jumping over the low, stone, dividing wall and pounding on the door. Vanya answered in her pyjamas, bouncing the baby, almost crying herself. David stepped onto the threshold and she stepped back. She looked into his eyes, questioning, pleading.

He took the baby from her and she said "No" or something like it. She held her arms out as he held the baby like a football above his head. The baby didn't stop crying. Vanya screamed the same word. "No", or "Please", maybe.

David threw the baby at the wall and screamed "Shut The Fuck Up". The baby was silent. Vanya dropped to her knees, wailing, gurgling "No". She picked the baby up. It was blue and floppy.

David's heart had pounded, like he'd just run a mile. His brain had felt like wire wool. He couldn't stop screaming. His vision became cloudy grey. The wire wool feeling gave way to an exquisite numbing pressure: a vice tightened by God or Jesus or all the fucking angels. The cherubim and the seraphim and the erelim.

He was awake. Sobbing. The tarp sizzled.

He knew they would send more Watchers, more dogs.

"Sinner," a tree said.

"Murderer."

"Fucking murdering cunt."

"Baby killer."

"Shut up."

"Child-killing cunt."

"Please."

"Oh. He was tired."

"Shut up."

"Poor David."

"Boo-fucking-hoo."

"Shut up." He covered his ears but it was no good.

# FRIDAY

## 1

Abi had left his room during the night. Soothing sunlight warmed his cheek. He threw the duvet back then piled his pillows against the head-board and lay back, rubbing the crust from his eyes. He stroked the mattress where she'd been, saw the dried sex stains and a long hair. He picked it up and held it to the morning light. It was red and curly. "How the fuck?" he said and let the hair fall to the floor.

He didn't see Abi or her friends in the bar. After a Scottish breakfast, which would see him right until dinner, he showered and packed the few things he'd needed during the night. He found his ring in his hip pocket and cringed. He'd have to stop drinking, one day.

He took the car through the town and Diane told him to turn left. "Right you are, flossy." She was a strict disciplinarian, Diane. "I only did it because she's shagging Tom, you know."

"If you say so."

"I was angry."

"You're always angry. How do you know – Gail – is sleeping with – Tom?"

"She's not having sex with me, is she?"

"That means nothing. In one hundred yards – turn left."

"What do you know, anyway?"

"I know you need to talk to – Gail – when possible. Turn left. The longer you leave it – the worse it will get."

The car climbed out of the glen up to a viewpoint overlooking Ben Nevis and the surrounding mountains. He sat for a long time with the window down, letting the sun and a soft breeze in, scanning the horizon.

He dug out the Love Symbol album and nodded his head to "Sexy MF".

"It's about you, this, Diane."

"Please do not flirt with me – Robert. Have you heard anything I've said?"

"Yes! Fucking hell. Who are you? My mum? Only my mum calls me Robert."

The road took him up Glen Mor, high above the southern shore of Loch Lochy and then across the Caledonian Canal just before Invergarry.

"Please phone – Gail – when possible."

"Okay! I'll phone her tonight." Three touring bikes flew past him as he climbed out of the town. "Bye," he sang, and flipped a couple of fingers their way. "I was angry," he told Diane.

"How do you think – Gail – feels right now?"

"You don't need to—"

"You know what she's capable of when she feels – lonely – and – isolated. You know what she does to herself."

"Don't you think I've thought about that? There's two people in this marriage, you know? I've tried to make her understand." Diane didn't say anything. "She's been doing it for ages. Before I came along. Not often. Just when things are really bad." She still didn't say anything. He thought about turning her off and on again.

"Go on."

He looked down at her. "I thought you weren't listening. She told me, one time, it's about releasing the pressure. Like a valve. I told her that's bollocks. I said, I'm there for you if you need help. But it doesn't do any good. Anyway, I need to sort my head out before I can help her with hers."

"What is the problem with your head?"

"You need to pay more attention, flossy. What have I been saying? She's leaving me. Piece by piece."

"Perhaps she feels – the same – about you."

He stopped again at a lay-by overlooking Loch Garry and Loch Loyne, stretched his legs. He was beginning to feel overwhelmed by the landscape. It

136

was not difficult to feel small among these lochs and mountains and he wasn't comfortable with the feeling. Against his will, he felt another pang of loneliness and wanted Gail in his arms. He wanted to tell her everything was going to be all right. That she didn't have to hurt herself anymore. Diane was right. She'd been right about everything so far.

As he met the dam at Loch Cluanie, he threw glances across the mountains to the south. Sunlight flooded the rich, green and brown patchwork and sparse clumps of pine nestled at the foot of the dam. The massif looked like a model; not a distant landscape but something smaller and more tangible.

"She's shagging Tom."

"You don't know that."

"I don't know what to do."

"Go straight ahead."

At Shiel Bridge he came to the sea. He was sure of it this time as there was a fishing boat bobbing about near the shore. He passed a warning sign that said FERAL GOATS and laughed. The road rolled like the fishing boat along the shore of Loch Duich.

"In two – hundred yards, turn right. Just tell her how you feel." He turned right at Auchtertyre and into the hills above Loch Alsh. As he wound down towards the next loch he passed a sign saying STROMEFERRY (NO FERRY), and laughed again.

The road hugged the coast and kept a single railway line company until a level crossing at Strathcarron. At Lochcarron – a row of houses and a school set back from the sea – he climbed again into the hills. Over to Shieldaig and Torridon.

At Kinlochewe, Diane told him to turn left. He was a bit sick of single-track roads, getting stuck behind Dutch camper vans that refused to pull over, and he asked her to take him to Ullapool by the fastest route.

"Good choice," she said.

"Thanks, Diane. You're all right, you. Very wise, for a sat nav."

"Thank you, Robert."

"Don't call me Robert."

The road immediately widened out, smooth and straight, and he flew past Loch a' Chroisg. The country around Loch Glascarnoch was more open than before – a bleak and brown plateau – but as he fell down towards Ullapool, the road became green with firs and silver birch.

"Well, Diane, I've enjoyed our little chat. I think it's going to be all right."

"You have reached your destination," Diane said.

## 2

Fraser sat at the kitchen table studying the drawing he'd made. He was writing a list of all the things he'd need from Airdrie's Hardware. It was the easy option to keep the boy confined to his room; sometimes he'd need something else to teach him a special lesson.

The cage would be made of softwood timber, screwed together with brackets. He'd need galvanized steel u-nails and a roll of wire netting. Some hinges and a padlock.

He'd thought about buying a puppy cage but it would be expensive and the boy would be able to lie down in it.

Fraser was still angry that the boy had made him leave the house, but he assured himself that his room would hold him until his return.

He folded the slips of paper and put them into the pocket of his sweatpants. He looked in his wallet and saw the fifty pounds there. He would need more than that if he was going to do a food shop as well. He put the wallet in his other pocket and felt its weight pulling his sweatpants. He swore and yanked at the wallet. His pocket turned inside out. He took his debit card from his wallet and picked up his car keys, placed the wallet back in the drawer.

He found himself whistling as he walked towards the front door. He hadn't had a little project like this for a while.

## 3

Ali watched Dad limping across the courtyard towards his car. He heard him whistling "Strangers in the Night". His heart pounded.

## 4

Gail left Annette and Lucy at the bar talking to some bloke they both knew. She took her pint out into the brilliant glow of the beer garden. The evening was warm and the wind had calmed. She found an empty picnic table and sat down. Her thigh was still stinging but she'd dressed it well and it was already healing. She moved the terracotta ashtray to another table, gulped her cider.

The girls soon appeared in the doorway and stretched their necks, trying to find her. She waved them over.

"I thought Tom was coming, anyways," Lucy said.

"He's playing squash with Anthony. They're coming later."

The conversation was subdued and polite until the fourth round kicked in and then they were shouting and laughing and screaming and hugging.

"I don't know what to do," Gail told them. "I just wish he'd come home." Her eyes brimmed with tears.

"Why don't you try phoning him again?" Lucy said.

"He'll just get angry and hang up again. He just shuts down on us when anything like this happens. He just won't talk to us. It's so frustrating."

"Well, if he won't come home," Annette said, "what if you go to him? You could fly up there in the morning, hire a car."

"Aye, pet," Lucy said, stroking her forearm.

"You know we had our honeymoon in the Orkneys? I didn't want to go but we had such a good time."

"Aye, I bet you did." The girls cackled.

"Not just that. Just the way we used to be. I want that back, you know?" She lifted her pint but it was empty. "You know how he proposed?"

"It was in the middle of the woods, wasn't it?"

"Aye, it was. In High Park Wood. But it was when he did it that's important. And I didn't know this until he told us a few years ago, right? He asked us on the tenth anniversary of him seeing us."

"Of yous meeting?"

"No of him seeing us. He saw us hanging about outside uni one day. Said the date was like etched on his mind."

The girls went "Aaaah" like someone had just walked in with a baby. Tom and Anthony rolled up then. Anthony caught up with the girls and Tom sat next to Gail at the picnic table.

"You okay?" he whispered, leaning into her.

She nodded and tried a smile. "I was just telling the girls about how me and Rob met," she said, her eyelids flashing. "How he proposed."

Tom nodded. "You all right for a drink?"

## 5

The boy would be hungry by now. He would put the timber and wire netting in the shed and then he'd make him some lunch. He looked up as he worked his way to the back of the car, the gravel crunching under his feet. The sun was warm behind the sparse, low cloud.

He felt something was awry when he neared the shed. His screwdriver was on the ground near the shed door. He would never have left it there himself. The boy must have been playing with it and not returned it to his tool box. Another issue he would have to raise tonight.

He stacked the timber and roll of wire in the corner of the shed. Again, a nagging feeling that something was amiss. Something about the shed just wasn't right. He closed the door behind him and padlocked the door.

As he climbed the stairs to the boy's room he could feel his absence. He pulled himself up the handrail and the tenth step creaked. He turned the corner on the landing and saw that the upper stairs were sparkling. Splintered glass littered the carpet. He craned his neck and saw shards of glass at the foot of the boy's door. He looked up. The glass from the transom window was gone. It had been picked clean.

Raged filled him. "Who's going to tidy this lot up now, eh?" He slammed his fist against the handrail. The bannister creaked and shook. "Who's going to tidy it up?"

Something about the shed wasn't right, and now the realisation stoked his rage: the boy's bike was gone.

## 6

The Alba Hotel in Ullapool was a large, old cottage on a row that looked down onto the harbour side. The bar had bare, stone piers, cream wallpaper with prints depicting old lairds. The floors were thick, tartan carpet or hardwood.

Rob finished his pint of Five Sisters then went to the bar to try another. The girl behind the bar – flat-faced with a nice bum – pulled a pint of Summer Isle.

"Where do people go to on a Friday night round here?" Rob said.

"Not here."

Rob laughed at that. He took the pint back to his table. It was a light, golden ale with a hint of honey. A window framed a high chimney stack on one of the lower houses against the grey-green mountains across the loch. A light rain had passed, leaving one side of the chimney dark, and it glinted in the pale dusk. He cringed at the memory of Rachel, stood at her sink with damp hands.

It was past eight but it was quiet. He looked around the room for something interesting. There were posters advertising what looked like a prog rock band called Quellerdrive. They were appearing the next night.

"Oh shucks. I will not be here," he droned.

A young, attractive couple, huddled together over coffee and guide books, glanced at him then continued to chammer away in Dutch or German. The girl's lips were pink and glossy. He picked up a beer mat, read it then looked up at the barmaid, who gave him a friendly smile. He sat back and pulled his wedding ring over his knuckle then made a fist.

The *Get Carter* theme rang in his hip pocket and he leaned over to get it. It was Gail. His chest lurched and he answered it.

"Hello?"

"Hello!" There was loud music playing. She must

be in the pub. "Rob, it's me."

"I know it's you. How you doing?"

"I want you to come home." She sounded drunk. Drunker than him, anyway.

"I'm coming home. In a few days."

"I'm lonely. I miss you." He didn't say anything to that. "Where are you now?"

"Er, Ullapool. It's a little town on the west coast. I'm driving up to John O'Groats tomorrow."

"Are you going to the Orkneys?"

"I don't know. I might."

"I could meet you there."

"At John O'Groats?"

"Aye." She must be drunk. She never said "Aye" when she was sober.

"You could do."

"You don't sound very enthusiastic." Her voice became fractured.

"I am. It's a good idea. How are you getting there?"

"I'll get the first flight tomorrow. I'll hire a car. When will you be there?"

"Say again? You're breaking up."

"When will you get there?"

"Erm. About lunchtime? We could meet in Thurso and get the ferry to Stromness."

"Aye. I'd really like that." He heard the chorus of "Wig Wam Bam" in the background. "Rob."

"What?"

"I love—" She was cut off. He looked at the phone. Then he typed a text: I love you too Gooey.

He pocketed the phone and looked around the

room as if expecting some kind of congratulations. Now he had a plan. He'd finish the pint of Summer Isle then he'd try and get through as many of the single malts behind the bar as possible.

## 7

The screaming moon hung bright in a clear, indigo sky, bright enough to cast shadows. His skin pallid, almost grey. His hair like an oversized black cap.

Tonight his sleep had been dreamless. He deserved that much. He looked forward to Thurso; he looked back at Thurso. Most years they'd catch the ferry to Stromness. Sometimes, just a day trip. They'd catch another ferry to Hoy and walk along the coast to the Old Man. David would say he wanted to climb it and his dad would tell him not to be silly. His mum would say that he could climb it when he was a wee bit bigger. He was maybe ten, the last time he went to the Orkneys. It would be nice to see the islands again. But Thurso was the important thing. He'd find peace there.

He heard the forest dozing. The trees stood round a large shallow bowl like mourners round a grave. They weren't very talkative tonight. He sat up and had a drink. The water felt cool all the way to his stomach. He rolled from under the tarp and stood, caressing the compass within his coat pocket. A deer at the other side of the bowl raised its head and stared at him before bounding off through the trees. In its place, five Watchers rose up, as if levitating. He dropped to his knees. They were staring into him. He looked around at his gear. It was scattered around in the blue darkness. He looked up and saw more Watchers join the others. A dog howled. The Watchers were silent; only their dogs made noise. His stomach felt loose. "No time." He grabbed his pack and his sleeping bag and threw dirt over the ashes of his fire. He crept away, hunched over his pack. Maybe they hadn't seen him after all.

"Maybe they were just guessing."

## 8

The sun had gone but it had left its warmth. Now the air felt dense. He'd asked her if she wanted to stay at his: it would be cheaper than a taxi out to Ponteland and he could drive her home in the morning. She'd agreed.

Tom's house was cool and smelled of fresh laundry. Gail sat on the hard, backless sofa and Tom put some music on.

"Drinks," he said and disappeared into the kitchen. She took her shoes off and rummaged in her bag for her lipstick.

"What is this?" she shouted. He didn't hear. She put her feet up, leaned on her elbow. Tom came back into the room with two gin and tonics. "What's this?"

"This? Ornette Coleman." He handed her a glass.

"It's a bit much, isn't it?" she said, taking a gulp.

"I suppose so," he smiled. "For a Friday night. I'll find something else." He went to the bookshelf and found the remote exactly where it should be. He scanned through his Artists list, selected something.

"Is this Billie Holliday?"

"No. Ella Fitzgerald." He took his drink to his easy chair opposite her. Ella Fitzgerald was singing a ballad she'd heard somewhere before.

"If I didn't know better, I'd say you were trying to seduce me, Tom Greenwood."

"What? No!" He looked genuinely shocked and she regretted saying it.

"I'm only kidding." She took another swig. "Jeez, Tom, how much gin have you put in here?"

"About a finger?"

"Have you met me?" She held up her glass.

"Two fingers?" he smiled, standing.

"Bit keen, but if you insist," she grinned. He took her glass and padded back into the kitchen. She let her feet drop and leaned forward to stand. Another song came on, another ballad. She quite liked her voice but she wasn't in the mood for any more of Tom's jazz. She scrolled down his Songs list and stopped at "Love Will Tear Us Apart", smiling. Tom came in then. "I didn't know you liked Joy Division, Tom."

"I like all sorts." He handed her the refilled glass and they clinked them together.

She took a gulp. "Let's have a dance," she said and moved closer to him, holding her glass high. She put her hand on his shoulder and he wrapped his arm around her waist, pulling her in. Their feet circled each other. She took another sip and put the glass on the shelf. He did the same and took her hand. He bowed his head and his breath was warm on her ear.

She felt herself getting wet. He murmured the chorus in her ear and she let go of his hand, latched it round his neck. She realised she'd buried her face into his chest and she could feel his hand moving down from the small of her back. She looked up and his eyes were ready to meet hers. She threw an instinctive glance at some point on the wall but then met his intense gaze again. Then he was kissing her. She didn't turn away; she didn't pull back. His lips were firm and cool from the gin and tonic. She felt his hand exploring her waist and then her breast. Her heart thumped. She felt his tongue flick into her mouth. She pushed away and pulled his shirt out as he worked on her zip. She felt herself wanting to say "Stop", felt the looming shame of her body. Her trousers slumped around her ankles and she stood stiff, waiting for his questions. He looked down at her body then pulled her in.

"You're beautiful," he whispered, and she stepped out of her trousers. Then he was picking her up and she was straddling him and giggling. She hooked her arms around his neck and he took her into his bedroom.

The song finished.

### 9

Fraser watched the oven clock change to 12:03. The phone kept ringing. He didn't want to jam up the emergency line. A young woman answered and sang: "Hello, Police. How can I help you?"

"Sergeant Maitland, please."

"Who is it I can say is speaking?"

"It's Fraser Byrne."

"And what's it regarding?" What did this bitch have to sing about?

"It's a personal matter, love. Is he there?"

"I'm afraid he's not on shift today. Do you want to leave a message?"

Fraser tried to keep his voice steady. "No, that's all right, darling."

"Do you not have his mobile number?"

"No. I lost it. You wouldn't happen to have –"

"Well I wouldn't be able to give you it over the phone but –"

"That's all right, darling." He cleared his throat. "I'd like to report a missing person."


## 10


Ali lay on his side on the mattress that smelled like a cellar, cradling and stroking his injured hand. He stared out at the horizon and saw a tanker come into view from the east. A milky sheet of altostratus cloaked the sky but for a ragged band of blue at the horizon. The sound of the waves below soothed him and he felt his eyelids drooping. In the morning he would ride his bike to Georgemas Junction and catch the first train to Inverness. By the time they found his bike at the station he'd be in Aberdeen.

Somewhere outside and above him, a gull squawked, and he flinched. The cave was dark even though the sun was still up. The tanker was in the middle of the uneven frame of the cave entrance now. He held his arm straight and shut one eye and squeezed the tanker between his finger and thumb.

He sat up and grimaced at the throbbing pain in his behind. He shone his torch into his school bag. He'd brought a tin of beans and sausages from the house but had forgotten the tin opener. He made crisp sandwiches and drank warm Irn Bru. Afterwards, he took stock. There was the rest of the loaf, a couple of apples and the chocolates that Dad had bought himself last Christmas. That would keep him going until he got to Aberdeen.

He looked through the wallet again. There was Dad's driving license, his credit card, some stamps and the money. He didn't know how much the train to Aberdeen would cost. He'd have enough to get to Inverness, though.

He took the cash, folded it twice and put it in his coat pocket. He shone the torch at the credit card; it was no good to him so he folded it in half and then back on itself until he could tear it. He threw the pieces and the wallet towards the back of the cave.

Then he pointed the torch towards the tanker and clicked the button off and on. S-O-S. He knew they wouldn't see it. The tanker was almost out of view, on its way to New York or somewhere.

He laid back and buried himself in his coat and stared up at the darkness and let his eyes close.

# SATURDAY

## 1

Gail was perched naked on the edge of Tom's bed, her feet at twenty to four. Her curtained forehead rested on her hand. She looked round at Tom; he was pretending to sleep. She stood and gathered her clothes, tiptoed downstairs. There was a sharp pain inside the top of her head. Her mouth tasted dirty. She pulled her clothes on, weeping. She wanted Rob to hold her. And she wanted to cut herself.

## 2

Northwest Sutherland, looking like another planet: bare hillocks and small lochs of liquid obsidian swathed in an invading, rolling fog from the sea. The road narrowed to a single track through rocky outcrops but traffic was sparse and he felt like he was doing sixty down a driveway.

Rob realised that his liver wasn't as efficient with whisky as with beer and there seemed to be something loose in his head. He didn't feel drunk but his eyes struggled to keep up with his brain, or the other way round. He drove with both windows down and "Purple Rain" at high volume.

He hoped for the road to widen at Durness but it slowed with oncoming traffic from the far side of Loch Eriboll. Here the fog gave way to a light rain and he welcomed the cooler air. He skirted the loch and the road widened and sped up. He dipped and switched through Tongue, Bettyhill and Strathy, past galleries and tea rooms. He slowed down through Reay. A dog barked at him as he passed. He barked back.

The metal cubes and white golf ball of Dounreay Power Station sat like occupying alien spacecraft. He watched them glide past as the car bounced along the road.

"Please – slow down," Diane said.

"Got to get there."

"You don't need – to rush. Gail's plane doesn't land until – twelve – oh six."

"I just want to get there. First important thing I've

done in fucking years."

"So take your time. Enjoy it."

"I just want to get there, Diane."

### 3

The golden land lay under high fleeting clouds. David looked down on the grey town below. He felt the calming smoothness of the compass casing. He'd left his map behind but he didn't need it now. He hadn't needed it at all. Thurso was now within his little circle of earth. This was farm land, the first he'd seen since the sun rose on the Black Isle.

A swarm of cleg-birds had followed him to the edge of the forest but no further. He slogged across the fields, enjoying the rhythm of the stone walls, heading north towards Scrabster. A cautious sense of serenity filled him. He saw seagulls cascading above the town. A tractor skirted the horizon, bothered by more gulls. He felt a cool relief at the life he was sensing all around.

The last plantation was receding, sinking behind him: a fading black shape like the memory of a bad dream. He looked back and saw movement there: a dark thread scintillating below the shadow of the trees. He smelled death, rotting meat. He looked back again and saw an army of Watchers spreading like a sepsis across the fields. David moaned. This was an army bent on destruction, annihilating the golden green of the earth. This was their last charge. There were no hounds; they had no need of them now. There was nowhere else for him to hide. He ran towards the town. The fields were large and flat and he found the going easy. The dry-stone walls were low and sturdy.

Soon, the dark green line of a road lay ahead of him. He looked back at the approaching army. It oozed from the forest like oil. He faltered over hard, dusty furrows. One more wall before the road. Here, the stones were loose; some had fallen from the wall. He planted a hand and threw his legs over.

## 4

Ali took the back roads away from the house, trying to stand on his pedals as much as possible. He didn't want anyone he knew seeing him so he stayed away from the town. The lanes took him past farms and disused quarries towards Newlands of Geise. He let the bike drop down a bank; the road swept to the left and the bend sharpened.

## 5

The land started to calm down. The car passed worked fields for the first time since Pitlochry. Rob was approaching Thurso and sunlight flooded through high, thin clouds onto Dunnet Head. The road raised him above the surrounding land. He passed through a heavy shower and the wipers slashed across the windscreen. Again, he wound the windows down and shouted along to "Kiss". He threw thumbs at oncoming lorry drivers.

He could see the sea trying to hide to his left. The road sank beneath the fields and narrowed between high grass verges. He saw warning signs but kept his speed up.

## 6

David felt the wall give way under his weight and heard something in his shoulder like a leg being ripped from a chicken. He screamed and fell with the disturbed stones down a high, steep verge towards the lane below. The stones spread out and rolled and bounced erratically across the road. David tumbled and hit his head on the tarmac. He righted himself and looked up to see a boy on a push bike. His wheel hit one of the stones; the bike wobbled and tipped him over. The boy cried out. David heard a car approaching. He sat at the foot of the verge, bruised and tender, weak and half-starved. He stared at the boy. A wee skinny blond laddie, damaged-looking. He was tangled up in the bike. The boy and the bike were the same thing.

"My leg," the boy-bike squealed.

David pushed himself to his feet, moaning. He limped over to the boy-bike and crouched down, touching the cool metal like a cautious rabbit.

The car was going too fast; the verges were too high. David heard the tyres scream and staccato blasts of the horn. He yanked the boy free of the bike and pulled him into the gutter. The back of the car swung towards them, bouncing and jolting over the scattered stones. David tried to pull the boy up the verge, planting his boots into the black mud of the gutter. The back of the car glanced off the boy's hip and thigh and David felt him wrenched from his arms.

The bike snagged itself under the car, anchored it to the road. David saw it come to a rest and the boy beyond, laying inert, halfway up the verge. He crawled towards him and heard the car door open. Gritty footsteps, then: "Fuck!"

The boy lay twisted on his back. David held his grimy cheek to the boy's face, felt his warm breath.

"Fucking hell fire!" The driver was pacing around the car.

A short, balding man in baggy jeans and a green tee shirt. He was holding his head and saying "Fuck". David could see his hairy belly peeking from under his shirt.

"Is he all right?" the driver said. David eased the boy onto his side. He stood and backed away, staring at the driver.

### 7

Ali saw the walker crumpled up at the bottom of the steep verge and he dropped to his saddle. He would remember that face for years after: the black, haunted eyes; the pallid skin. Like a ghost. He leaned away from the walker but his back tyre slid from under him. The ground yanked him off his bike. Then he heard something snap and felt raw, burning pain as his bare legs and arms grated across the road surface. He felt very dizzy and he lost control of his eyes for a few seconds then the walker was crouching over him. He heard tyres screeching and then a car horn. The walker pulled him up and he screamed as he felt the bike falling away and banging against his leg.

He could feel the walker's wiry arms tight around his chest then they were both falling onto the grassy verge.

Ali watched the car skid over the bike and then judder to a stop. Then pain in his hip. He felt like he was flying, or falling. Again, dizziness, then darkness.

When he came round the walker was gone and another man in shorts and a tee shirt was crouched next him. "Are you okay?" he said. "Stay still."

## 8

He kicked the brake, heard a skid and felt the car lurch to the left. He relaxed his foot. He was still going too fast. He squeezed the brake again. A dark figure was crouching over the boy. The car slowed but the road was wet and again he started to spin to the left. He tried to keep the car pointing forward but turned the wrong way and made it worse. He yanked the wheel back round but it was too late. The dark man was heaving at the boy. He didn't seem able to move him. Still the car moved sideways along the road. The dark man was dragging the boy out of the way, free of the bike. They were both staring at him with wild, pleading eyes. The dark man pulled the boy off the road and fell back. Rob's car was almost going backwards now. It juddered over the bike before bouncing up the verge into a wall, sending stones spilling onto the road. The side airbag burst open and he bounced off it, hitting his knee against the partition. "Fuck." His feet slipped from the pedals and the car lurched forward before stalling. He sat dazed for a moment. His stomach felt tight and his head hurt. "Fuck!" He squeezed the steering wheel. Prince was still singing. He looked to his right; his neck tightened and he moaned. He saw the boy lying on the verge at the other side of the road. He was looking at him. He couldn't see the dark man.

He opened the door and limped straight towards the boy. "Are you okay?"

"Aye. My leg hurts."

"Where did you come from?"

"I fell off."

"Who was that man?"

"I don't know."

"Are you hurt?"

"My leg."

"Okay. Er, don't move. I'll phone the police."

"No."

"Eh?"

"Don't phone them. I'll be right." He tried to stand and yelped, dropped back down to his elbows.

"Stay still. I'm going to get help." He looked round for the bike. It must still be under his car. He took his phone out and dialled 999. "Ambulance." He looked down at the boy. "Stay still. You're going to be all right."

## 9

"...usual things orange uncertainty I don't know yet maybe things who undo usual money by line by grade things that may enquire retic retic reticular usual world came to ownership of many things that haven't been untold actualist calm setter usual things unpresidential two hands which world came and cone litigation sensors things that don't continue without outspoken orange uncertainty usual things I don't know orange uncertainty two hands which world came things that may enquire reticular usual world came to litigation sensors ownership of things that haven't been untold actualist calm setter usual things by line by grade and cone things that don't continue yet maybe things who undo usual money without outspoken unpresidential orange uncertainty things who undo usual money usual things I don't know yet maybe things that may enquire retic reticular usual world actualist came to ownership of many litigation orange uncertainty things that haven't been untold calm setter unpresidential usual things two hands which world came and cone sensors things don't continue without outspoken orange uncertainty by line by grade..."

David limped across the fields towards Thurso.

## 10

It was too early to check in. The lobby of The McCallan Hotel in Thurso was also the bar. Gail took a sip of coffee to wash down the last of her muffin and sat back in an upholstered wing chair. It was comfortable – enough for her to think about having a nap – but the cream-and-crimson tartan didn't go with the blue and green of the carpet. She hid behind her sunglasses, watching a few local men drinking lager and reading papers. Guests came and went. Her eyes felt tight from crying and fatigue.

She'd left Tom sleeping and whispered for a taxi. Back in Ponteland she showered with the thought of a nice shiny razor blade flashing like a strobe while the hot water washed away her tears. There was a flight to Wick at 9:40 via Aberdeen. She arrived at midday and drove to Thurso in her hire car.

She looked through a large square window onto houses and shops of grey stone and greyer pebble-dash. The sun faded in and out from behind fleeting, purplish clouds. She hadn't seen much of the town the last time they were here. She hadn't missed much.

She wondered where Rob would be and thought about calling him. She'd already texted him to say she'd arrived. And then a pang of guilt stabbed at her stomach. It couldn't happen again. She was meeting Rob and they were going to sort all this out – have a good talk about everything. But it was Rob who'd started this. (She rebuked herself – started it, as if they were children.) But he'd had sex with plenty of others before she'd done the same last night. And it wasn't like Rob with his prostitutes. She and Tom were friends. She felt her cheeks burning and her eyes stinging as she dabbed away more tears.

The first time, Rob had gone into Newcastle for a curry. He'd phoned and told her he was staying at Craig's house. He never stayed out and would especially never stay at Craig's. It would be as easy to come home. Gail phoned Craig's house, knowing on some deep level that Rob wouldn't be there, not having an excuse to phone if he was there. Craig's fiancée Emma answered the phone saying that Craig was working away that weekend. And Gail had hung up without saying thank you or goodbye.

She squirmed in her chair and her phone rang. The screen said number withheld.

"Hello?" she sniffed.

"Hello, is this Gail Gibson?"

"Yes."

"This is PC Davies from Highlands and Islands Police calling. Are you the wife of a Robert Gibson?"

"Yes, I am. What's wrong?"

"There's no need to worry, Mrs Gibson, but Rob's been involved in a road traffic collision. He's been taken to Dunbar Hospital." Gail stared with glassy eyes. "Hello? Mrs Gibson?"

## 11

The doctor didn't look like a doctor. If it wasn't for the stethoscope around his neck, Ali would've thought he was in a band or he was a student. He had black, spiky hair and black shoes, brothel creepers, they were called. He wore an old-looking, short-sleeved shirt, not tucked in, and he had a silver ring that made a hole in his ear lobe.

"Alistair Byrne," he said as he spun around the curtain. Ali propped himself up on his elbows but tried not to move around on the bed too much; he didn't want to tear the paper.

"Aye."

"Just lie back and relax. What shall I call you?"

"Everyone calls me Ali."

"Hello, Ali, I'm Doctor Pryce." Ali watched him as he looked at the clipboard with all his notes on and then at his watch. "You've been here a while, Ali. Has anyone phoned your parents?"

"My dad's away. He works on the rigs."

"I'm just going to examine your leg, Ali. I'll need to take your shorts off. What about your mum?"

"She – she's at work."

"Do you have her work number?"

"I don't know it."

"Try to wiggle your toes. Where does she work?"

"Er."

"That's fine. You can relax now."

"I can't remember."

"All right, Ali. No bother. We're going to have to give you an X-ray. See what sort of damage you've got to your leg. But at this stage it looks like it's broken so we'll have to put a cast on, I'm afraid."

"Right."

"The paramedic said you had some back pain as well."

"Aye."

"All right, can you sit up and take your tee shirt off and I'll have a wee keek?"

"It's no bother. It's only bruised."

"Well, I'm going to have to examine you to see if it's any more serious than that." Ali sat up and pulled at the collar of his shirt. "Shall I give you a hand?"

"No."

"All right." Ali looked at a spot on the paper between his feet but he could feel Doctor Pryce looking at him. He felt his face warming as he pulled his tee shirt over his head. "It looks like it's brightening up out there, young Ali." Doctor Pryce side-stepped behind Ali and touched his shoulders. Ali flinched. "It's all right, wee man. Try to relax." Doctor Pryce pressed his fingers up and down his backbone and Ali stiffened. "Did you hurt your back before you were knocked down, Ali?"

"No."

"Right." He sounded puzzled. "They don't look like bruises you'd normally get from—" Ali didn't hear the rest. There was a commotion in the corridor: raised voices. Then, as if he'd been standing there the whole time, he heard Dad's paper and comb voice at the other side of the curtain. Ali felt sick, then his shorts were warm and wet. He could feel Doctor Pryce looking at him and he pulled the blanket over his lap. The curtain billowed open. Dad stood at the foot of the bed. There were two nurses behind him. Ali stared at the spot on the paper.

"How is he?" Dad murmured.

"I'm sorry. Who are you?" Doctor Pryce said.

"I'm the boy's father."

"Oh." Again, he sounded puzzled. "Well, Ali's been knocked down. He's got quite a serious injury to his leg."

"You can't keep him here if I don't want you to, though, can you?"

"Well, the thing is, because you didn't bring Ali in—"

"It's Alistair. His name's Alistair."

"Okay. Because you didn't bring Alistair in, sir, you're going to have to show us some ID."

"I'm his father."

"I've no doubt of that, sir. It's just a formality. If you want to go back outside and show Linda, the receptionist, some form of ID. Then I can give you a full run down of Ali-stair's injuries."

For the first time Ali looked up at Dad's face. He was staring with wide, glossy eyes at Doctor Pryce. The doctor was staring back.

"I don't have my wallet."

"Well. I'll tell you what, sir. I'll start treating Alistair's injuries while you pop home for your wallet. How's that?"

"Are you fucking kidding me? I'm his father. Alistair, tell him I'm your father." Ali looked at the spot.

"All right, all right," Doctor Pryce said. "Do you want to try to keep nice and calm, sir? Like I say, I've no doubt what you're saying is true but we need to be sure. It's more than my job's worth to let you take him out of the hospital if we don't make it official, okay?" He was still looking Dad straight in the eye. "Do you understand?"

"Aye, I understand." Ali glanced and saw Dad staring at him. "Well. I'll be back later on. He belongs at home with his father."

Doctor Pryce took hold of the curtain. "Of course he does, sir." Dad stepped back and Doctor Pryce drew the curtain. Ali stared at the curtain. It was a bluey green with a swirly pattern. He thought he'd seen the pattern before but he didn't know where.

"I thought everyone called you Ali."

Ali looked down at the balled-up blanket, gathered it up and offered it to the doctor. He could only stare at it.

"Don't worry about the blanket, Ali. We'll get you cleaned up."

Doctor Pryce called for the nurses and they came round the curtain. They took the blanket and his jeans and pants and gave him a hospital gown then helped him move to another booth while they cleaned up. The doctor was quiet while he examined Ali's back. Finally he said: "Who did this to you, Ali?"

Ali looked up at Doctor Pryce, who was looking down at him with the same look as that walker had. The same look that Mum had given him sometimes. His vision blurred and he felt tears spilling from his eyes. His voice was a broken, ragged whisper.

## 12

The town felt like an old friend, like the father he'd never had. Old and grey, handsome under the high sun. The feeling of calm made his insides buzz.

He washed himself in the Public Conveniences on the High Street. The soap came out of the dispenser already foamed. He stared at it in the middle of his palm. It smelled of lavender. Men stared at his half-naked, battered body but he didn't care. His shoulder throbbed; he had difficulty lifting his arm but he didn't think it was dislocated.

Whatever happened next would happen. The Watchers held the hills. The humans were less predictable but safer. He might expect a firm hand on his shoulder as he sat on a park bench or a friendly greeting as he looked at a shop window. Then he would feel the cleansing flood of relief, of absolution.

He left the toilets and followed the smell of vinegar to a fish shop. A police car filed towards him in the midday traffic and he bowed his head and rubbed his scalp as it passed. He looked back; there was no sign of them seeing him. He checked his thigh pockets. One was still packed with screwed up tens and twenties. The notes were crinkled and stiff after being soaked and dried again. He ordered two portions of fish and chips, one closed, one open. He splashed vinegar all over them then stuffed chips into his mouth. He put his change in the collection box for kiddies with cerebral palsy. The lady said "Thanks" and made a big thing out of it with the man who was frying the fish. He must've given her a tenner.

David scooped up his food and left. He decided to walk down to the sea. Tomorrow he might catch the ferry to Stromness, start a new life. Maybe he'd do some sea fishing when he got there. He still had his flint and his sleeping bag but he'd have to buy a new knife and fishing line. Maybe he could build a new home on Rousay, plant a small vegetable garden.

He walked down a back street, sucking up large pieces of haddock. He came to a window and looked inside. It wasn't a shop window. It was a small room with no visible door and it was carefully arranged with old things. Things from the war: a gas mask, some bullets. A rag doll, a spinning top, model cars, lead soldiers, rusty tins, tea caddies. On the side wall there were old metal Ovaltine and Bovril signs. A frilly lampshade hung low from a dark ceiling. David saw a button on the window frame with a little sign saying PRESS FOR LIGHT. He pressed it and the room glowed orange like there was a piece of time trapped in there.

He picked out other things: old cigarette cards, a gramophone at the back, old books, chipped water jugs with different whisky labels. He stepped back, smiling. A small, metal box was fixed to the stone cill. Another wee sign said: DONATIONS WELCOME. David folded a twenty the best he could and slipped it into the box. He shaded his eyes and looked back through the window. He pressed the button. The room glowed and he scanned the scene again. This time he saw a thing he'd missed before. Tucked into a wooden wine crate was an old, balding doll. One of her eyes was shut. He stared at the doll until the light went out.

He dabbed his eyes with his sleeve but it was too late. He heaved in a sob and folded to the ground. He found himself leaning against the wall under the window, his half-eaten fish and chips crumpled in his lap. He shaded his eyes as if this would keep the tears in. He heard people passing, felt their stares.

Finally, a woman's voice. "Can I help you?" Foreign. Maybe German. He looked up and pushed himself off the pavement, leaving the fish and chips. "Are you okay?" He turned away and staggered off to find somewhere to sleep.

## 13

The Granville Bar was a short walk from the hotel. There were three or four small rooms trapped in the 1980s, with a television in each, all showing Celtic in some international away game. There were radiators on the walls and lino on the floors. The air was warm and stale. Rob and Gail sat side by side in silence, with a pint and half of lager in front of them.

Rob had spent the morning in the local hospital. The X-rays and CT scan were clear but his knee was still tender, and the doctor had suggested paracetamol for the headache. The police had breathalysed him at the scene and asked him some questions. He'd said he was doing below sixty when he saw the man and boy in the lane. Maybe he was. With no witnesses, they had to take his word for it. The car was a write-off; the front axle had been bent and couldn't be driven.

Gail had met him at the hospital.

Now they sat sipping their drinks and people-watching. A tall, thin man stood like a sentry near the door holding a pint and half of Guinness. He wore a black shirt and tie and his ears were mainly lobes. A well-dressed man entered the pub, or at least at first sight he was well-dressed. Looking closer and longer, Rob saw that his blue linen suit was crumpled and his grubby, white shirt collar was curled up. His purple paisley tie looked second-hand years ago. The man behind the bar said: "You going to behave tonight, Gordon?"

Gordon said: "Pint of lager, please, young James." James poured Gordon his drink and Gordon took a long draught, nearly half the glass. He looked around the bustling bar and reached into his inside jacket pocket, brought out a pack of darts. A woman at the other side of the bar said "Gordon!" as if she was chastising a naughty puppy. Gordon took out a dart and started swinging his arm as if he was shaking a bottle of ketchup. Most of the people in the bar ducked and crouched before Gordon launched the dart indiscriminately towards one of the walls.

"Fuck!" barked a large, shaven-headed man over the confused din that was swelling through the pub. The dart had hit him on the nape of his neck. The bear of a man swung round and glared at Gordon, who was now swinging another dart. The bear man carefully put his pint on a table then dropped to the floor. Gordon lobbed another dart and it bounced off the clock above the bar. Everyone was now on the floor, shouting and screaming for Gordon to stop. Gordon ignored them; he had one more dart left.

Rob and Gail lay prone on the side bench. Gail was giggling like a schoolgirl. Gordon threw the dart like he was throwing bread to ducks and it embedded itself in the ceiling. "Get him!" someone shouted and the bear man rose up and launched himself at Gordon's midriff. People were back on their feet and Rob and Gail stood and followed some of the locals laughing and swearing out into the warm night.

Rob had his arm around Gail. He pulled her in and rested his chin on her shoulder, holding her head to his chest. She looked up at him.

"I'm sorry," he said as the locals milled around them. She smiled sadly and wrapped her arms around his waist. He could feel her crying into his shirt. He held her tight. "It's going to be better from now on."

The bear man and another were carrying Gordon out of the pub. James followed.

"You're barred, Gordon. For life. Get yourself home." Gordon patted himself down and walked down the street with all the dignity of the Queen. Rob limped back to the hotel with his arm around Gail's shoulder.

# SUNDAY

## 1

It was a new day. The sky was pure. Last week was another world.

David watched the wet sand dry with each bare footfall. He carried his jacket under his good arm and his trousers were rolled up to his knees. The sun warmed his head and face despite the breeze from Dunnet Bay. The tide was out and the beach was a wasteland. Ahead, the western cliffs of Dunnet Head rose from the sea. The ghostly islands beyond.

He thought he could find peace in Thurso. He found good fish and chips and an even better Scottish breakfast. Maybe he could find peace here instead. The further north the better. The high cliffs and his beloved islands. The end of all things.

## 2

Dad didn't come back that night. Ali had the deepest sleep he could remember, in spite of the pain in his leg. He awoke to the sound of coughing. The bed was strange to him but it was big and soft and the bedding was clean and smelled nice. He had three pillows and a crisp white sheet to cover him. The nurse, who was called Charlotte, had folded up the blankets and taken them away because the ward was so hot.

He looked around the ward. There were similar blue-green curtains to yesterday. The windows were tall and let in lots of light. A big rainbow was painted on the far wall with little cartoon farm animals dancing around underneath. The boy in the other bed was doing the coughing. He must have been brought in during the night. Ali didn't recognise him. Maybe he went to Mount Pleasant.

"All right?" he said. The boy coughed and nodded back. Ali stretched out his arm and picked up the copy of *Harry Potter and the Philosopher's Stone* that Nurse Charlotte had brought for him. He'd read it before but it was better than nothing. A hunger pang irked his stomach. Doctor Pryce had promised eggs and bacon for breakfast.

They'd had a chat just before he'd gone to bed. About his back and his hand and everything else. Everything. The words had left him like exorcized ghosts. He'd asked Doctor Pryce not to phone the police. Doctor Pryce said he would have to, said something about duty of care. He'd asked if there was anyone else he could stay with.

"My auntie. Auntie Fiona. In Aberdeen."

"Do you know where she lives?"

"No. Just Aberdeen."

"What's your auntie's last name?"

"McPherson."

"Okay, Ali. Leave it with me. Get some rest."


## 3

Gail drove and Rob stretched his leg out. It was only bruised but it was painful to move.

They hadn't had the talk yet.

They'd decided over breakfast to drive to John O'Groats on the way back to Wick Airport. There wouldn't have been enough time to enjoy the Orkneys anyway, Gail had said. The best laid plans of pissed up mice and men.

At Castletown, Rob looked over the wide beach of Dunnet Bay, blue under the green cliffs beyond. "Have a look at that."

She glanced past him. "Nice."

"We could go over there. That's the most northerly point on the British mainland, you know. Most people think it's John O'Groats but it's actually Dunnet Head."

"Will we have time?"

"It'll only take half an hour."

"We don't want to miss the plane."

"Well, if you'd rather go to John O'Groats that's fine."

"It'd be nice to go back."

He looked down at her thighs. He'd seen the new scars last night. He'd asked her when she'd done it and she'd changed the subject.

Now he looked at her and stroked her other thigh. "You won't need to hurt yourself again, Gooey." He looked across the bay. "Ever."

She glanced at him and smiled. "Can we wait until we get home?" Another glance. "I don't want to start crying while I'm driving."

## 4

It was a matter of waiting now. The boy must've told that scruffy cunt of a doctor everything. All about the family's business. Private business. Fraser had dug out the gas bill and was about to leave the house for the hospital. But then he'd closed the door, gone to the kitchen for his whisky and sat at the kitchen table. He knew that wee slut on reception wouldn't take a gas bill as ID. And even if she did, Gary, or worse, some young constable who he didn't know, would be there waiting.

"Let's face it." He had failed in his raising of the boy. He wanted to blame his wife but "Who am I kidding?" Who else? His father? All he got from him was a funeral to pay for out of his first month's pay.

There was a sharp rattle of knocks at the door. He pushed himself up, smirking. He swung the front door wide and Gary and some young constable who he didn't know turned towards him.

"Fraser Byrne."

"Gary! To what do I—"

"Fraser Byrne. I am arresting you on suspicion of the rape of a young child under Section 18 of the Sexual Offences Act, 2009. You do not have to say anything. However, it may harm your defence if you do not mention when questioned something which you later rely on in court. Anything you do say may be given in evidence."

## 5

The house was in Pennyland, right behind his school. It was smaller than Dad's but full of life. A social worker had picked him up from the hospital. Esther, she was called. She'd said he would have a lot of fun at Carol and Sam's house. They had two kids of their own – they went to the high school – and a foster daughter who was six. Ali asked if he could just stay in his room and Esther said that it shouldn't be a problem.

The alarm clock on the bedside drawers said 21:37. The last of the sun flooded the room in golden light. There was a television in the room but he wasn't really watching it. He leaned against the window cill on his good leg and stared across the fields. The barley rippled along a low, darkening hillside. A fuzzy smudge over the sea was the only cloud. Cirrus uncinus.

There was a soft knock. Ali's heart lurched. He pushed away from the window cill and saw Carol peeking around the door. "Alistair, you've got a visitor." For a second, he thought it might be Dad. "It's only Esther." Ali took up his crutches from the bed and lurched towards the door; Carol smiled and stepped back as she ushered him out.

Esther was sat in one of the leather armchairs in their Big Room. Carol showed him in. "I'll give you a wee bit of privacy, eh?" She backed out of the room, closed the door behind her.

"Hello, Alistair. How are you?" Esther said. She was leaning on a large, orange file.

"All right."

"Good. Sorry it's a bit late. I didn't wake you, did I?"

"No."

"It's been a bit hectic today. What have you been up to? Much? Come and sit down."

"Just watching a bit of telly."

"Great. You all right on your crutches? It's taken a while but I've made some headway in tracking down your auntie in Aberdeen." Ali nodded. She looked a bit nervous. "And I've got some bad news for you."

"Right."

"Ali, she died last year."

"Oh." He thought he might have to go back home and live with Dad.

"But the thing is that your mum's been living with her since she left Thurso."

"My mum's dead."

Esther slumped onto the file. "Is that what your

dad told you?" She seemed cross when she said that. "No, Ali. She's not." Ali saw her eyes were filling up. "She's still living in your auntie's house and she wants you to come and live with her."

Ali smiled, blinking. He felt like crying too.

## 6

The cliffs rose steadily from the sea and then the land undulated in a large curve round to the north. Across the bay to the west, Thurso went about its business. He felt more alone now than he had in his entire life. But not lonely. Just him, the wind, the screeching gulls. The breeze did nothing to quell the sun's heat. He threw his coat to the ground. These were the last effulgent miles of his journey. From somewhere lost inside him, a feeling of beatific joy arose. At the top of a knoll he saw the dark green islands like passing leviathans. It was the most beautiful thing he'd ever seen.

He climbed a wall into the grounds of the lighthouse and walked the last few yards to the edge of the cliff. The sun and the breeze on his face, cooling and warming. Somewhere, music played. Old, beautiful music.

Maybe tomorrow he'd catch the ferry to Stromness.

# AFTER

## 1

Gail woke up and felt his erection rubbing against her lower back. She felt his hand sliding over her hip and between her thighs. She raised her knee and let him play with her till she started getting wet. She half-turned and wrapped an arm around his neck; he kissed her and she was half-conscious of her morning breath. She twisted around onto her back and he clambered over her leg. He slid himself inside her and let out a whispered moan. God, she'd missed this. Missed him. She didn't want to stop kissing him. She pulled him in and lifted her legs, pointed her toes at the walls.

An image of Tom flashed onto the back of her eyelids: standing, unwavering, lifting her up and down as she clamped herself onto him, feeling his cock deep inside.

She felt Rob going limp and there was a flash of panic as she thought he was reading her mind. He pulled himself out, rolled onto his back.

Gail rolled with him and rubbed his chest. "It's okay."

He nodded, staring at the ceiling. She put her head on his shoulder and they lay there for a while. A yellow sliver from the broken slat on the blinds warmed her neck.

"Let's move to Scotland," he said.

"We could do."

## 2

Fraser had been waving at the CCTV camera in his detention cell. He'd been shouting too but he knew they couldn't hear him. He looked round the room. It was very clean and tidy. Nothing sticking out, no sharp corners. It was a while before anyone came. That was good.

Gary slid the hatch open. "What do you want, Fraser?"

"Gary, I need to talk to you."

"Are you sure you want to do that without your solicitor?

"Gary, we go way back, pal. Can you not do something?"

"What do you think I'll be able to do for you?"

"There must be something – "

"There's nothing," Gary shouted; then hissed: "I can do for you. I've done enough for you already. I should have done something years ago. Before Sarah left you. I can't turn a blind eye this time." Gary gave him a look halfway between pity and disgust. "The things he's told us."

"You don't understand, Gary. You've not got kids. I was just disciplining the boy."

"Shut up, you sick bastard."

"Gary, please. He's all I've got."

"Shut up. I don't want to hear it." He looked Fraser up and down. "Try to get some sleep." Gary slid the hatch shut. Fraser was trembling. He really was all he had. And now they'd taken him away from him. He sat on the edge of the bed. He wiped his forehead with his tee shirt. He wished he could open a window.

Gary had turned a blind eye one last time. There was no way he couldn't have noticed just because his back was turned. He knew Gary too well. He had a keen eye for detail, just like his old mate Fraser. He pulled his shoe laces out of his jeans pocket.

### 3

The fields spun past. Ali hadn't travelled this road since Mum had been there. They used to drive to Aberdeen most Christmases to see Auntie Fiona and Granny McPherson. She was probably dead too.

He looked through the windscreen, past Esther, at the mountains. The only mountain he'd seen in seven years was Morven, when he'd ridden his bike south, last summer.

"We can stop near Inverness, if you want," Esther said. "Get a picnic. Then we can take the scenic route through the Cairngorms. It's beautiful this time of year. Have you ever been there, Ali?"

"No. We went to Culloden once."

"Aye, that's just down the road. What do you fancy for your picnic?"

"An apple."

"An apple? Don't you want a sandwich?"

"Aye. And an apple."

"Right enough," she smiled.

The road swung down towards Cromarty Firth, wide and calm under the noon sun. He saw fishing boats at anchor and the low hills of the Black Isle beyond.

"Why did Mum leave me behind?" he said and turned to Esther.

She looked shocked. "Oh, Ali. I don't think it was like that. She needed to get away. She had no idea that your dad would hurt you like he did her."

"How do you know?"

"I had a long talk with her when I tracked her down. She was upset something awful." She checked her mirrors. "Tell you what, I bet she'll tell you everything you want to know when you get there." Ali nodded and looked out across the Firth. The bridge was looming into view. "Just try not to be too angry with her."

"I'm not angry with her," he said. The road swung round to the left, onto the bridge. There was a crash barrier but no pavement. A man in hiking gear was working against the flow of traffic; cars and lorries were sounding their horns and swerving out to avoid hitting him. He looked lonely, like the walker who pulled him off the road. Ali hoped he was going to meet someone.

## 4

SCOTTISH AMBULANCE SERVICE
TRANSCRIPT OF CASE NO. 9384131
CALL HANDLER: David Prudhoe (DP)
COMPLAINT DESCRIPTOR: pysch pt, violent
CALLER: 2nd party
DATE: [29/07/12]
CALL TIME: [04:37]

TRANSCRIPT TEXT
DP: Ambulance service, what's the address of the emergency?
Caller: My boyfriend's going mad. He's smashing the house up.
DP: I need the address of the emergency first of all.
Caller: It's [OMITTED]
DP: And what's your postcode?
Caller: [OMITTED]
DP: Just confirm the address.
Caller: What?
DP: Just give me the address one more time.

Caller: It's [OMITTED]

DP: And what town is that in?

Caller: [OMITTED]

DP: What's your phone number?

Caller: Oh, hurry up.

DP: What's your phone number?

Caller: [OMITTED]

DP: Okay. Tell me exactly what happened.

Caller: He's going crazy. He's gone mental. Please hurry up.

DP: Listen, caller. Help has been arranged. Try to keep calm. I need to ask you some questions. It's not going to delay the help. Are you with him now?

Caller: Aye. Can't you hear him? He's having some kind of – [OMITTED], please. No. Don't. Please.

DP: Listen to me. Don't shout at him. Try to keep calm so he keeps calm. How old is he?

Caller: Thirty-eight. Fuck, he's cut himself. His arm.

DP: Is he awake?

Caller: Aye.

DP: Is he breathing?

Caller: Aye, course he's fucking breathing.

DP: Listen, you need to keep calm so he keeps calm.

Caller: Okay.

DP: How has he cut himself?

Caller: [OMITTED], please, no. My baby's in the house. I need the police as well. Please come quickly.

DP: How has he cut himself?

Caller: He's smashed up the coffee table. He's cut himself on the glass. How long is it going to be?

DP: We're coming as fast as we can. Does he have a weapon?

Caller: No. No.

DP: Where is he now?

Caller: He's in the front room.

DP: Is this a suicide attempt?

Caller: No. I don't know. No. [OMITTED].

DP: Is he thinking about committing suicide?

Caller: I don't know. Fuck, there's blood everywhere.

DP: Try to keep calm, caller. I'll give you some instructions to control the bleeding soon. Is he completely alert?

Caller: No. Please come. [OMITTED]. No. Please don't. Put her down [OMITTED]. No.

DP: Hello. Hello. What's happening? What's [OMITTED] doing? Hello. Hello.

Caller: [Inaudible, caller screaming] My baby. He's thrown my baby. [OMITTED]. No.

DP: Where is the baby now?

Caller: He's thrown my baby. He threw her against the wall. No. [Inaudible, caller screaming]

DP: Caller, stay calm. What's your name? Tell me your name.

Caller: [OMITTED]. No. No. [OMITTED].

DP: Caller, stay calm so we can help her. Your name's [OMITTED]?

Caller: No.

DP: Caller, what is your name?

Caller: [OMITTED].

DP: [OMITTED]. Keep calm so we can help her. Where's [OMITTED] now?

Caller: He's outside. He's gone.

DP: Right, [OMITTED]. Take the phone to where your baby is.

Caller: [Inaudible, caller screaming] No. [Inaudible] She's gone blue.

DP: [OMITTED], keep calm so we can help her. Take the phone over to your baby.

Caller: Right.

DP: Are you next to her now?

Caller: Aye.

DP: Right. How old is she?

Caller: She's nine months.

DP: Okay. Is she awake?

Caller: No.

DP: Is she breathing?

Caller: She's all floppy.

DP: Is she breathing?

Caller: [Inaudible] No. Oh no.

DP: Listen to me [OMITTED]. You need to keep calm so we can both help [OMITTED].

Caller: [OMITTED].

DP: Keep calm so we can help her.

Caller: [OMITTED].

DP: Keep calm so we can help her. Okay, listen carefully [OMITTED]. Lay [OMITTED] flat on her back on the floor.

Caller: She's on her back.

DP: Okay. Kneel next to her, look in her

mouth for any vomit.

Caller: [OMITTED].

DP: Stay calm [OMITTED], you're doing really well. Is there anything in her mouth?

Caller: No.

DP: Okay. Now place your hand on her forehead, your other hand under her neck and shoulders, then slightly tilt her head back.

Caller: Okay.

DP: [OMITTED]. Put your ear next to her mouth. Can you feel or hear any breathing?

Caller: No.

DP: [OMITTED], stay nice and calm for me. You're doing really well because you're listening to me, right? Listen to me now, okay? I'm going to tell you how to give mouth to mouth.

Caller: Oh God.

DP: [OMITTED], keep listening to me. You're doing really well. With her head tilted back, completely cover her mouth and nose with your mouth then blow two puffs of air into the lungs, about one second each, just enough to make her chest – just enough to make the chest rise with each breath. Okay, have you done that?

Caller: Aye.

DP: Right. Did you feel the air going in and out?

Caller: Aye.

DP: Listen carefully, I'll tell you how to do resuscitation. Place two fingers on her breastbone in the centre of her chest, right between her nipples. Okay? Push down one inch with only your fingers touching the chest. Pump her chest hard and fast thirty times at least twice per second. Let the chest come up all the way between pumps. And tell me when you're done. Do you understand me so far?

Caller: Aye. Hello? Hello?

[At this point, DP leaves the call. Team leader Carolyn Corrigan (CC) takes over]

CC: Hello?

Caller: Hello.

CC: Are you pumping her chest, darling?

Caller: Aye.

CC: Remember, thirty times, okay?

Caller: Twenty-seven, twenty-eight, twenty-nine, thirty.

CC: Well done. You're doing really well. Right, my love, with your hand under her neck and shoulders, slightly tilt her head back again. Put your mouth over –

Caller: She's started breathing.

CC: She has, darling?

Caller: Aye, she's breathing.

CC: Right. Has she woken up?

Caller: No.

CC: Okay. Well I want you to tell me every time she takes a breath.

Caller: Now. Now.

CC: Keep going.

Caller: Now. Now.

CC: Okay, that's fine, darling.

Caller: [OMITTED]. Wake up, [OMITTED].

CC: Okay. [OMITTED]?

Caller: Wake up.

CC: [OMITTED], don't worry about waking her up, darling. I just want you to stay right with her, make sure her head's tilted back and keep checking her breathing. If she vomits, turn her onto her side and clean out her mouth and nose. I'm going to stay on the line until help arrives, okay? So tell me when the ambulance crew's there with her, or if anything changes. Okay? Okay [OMITTED]?

Caller: Okay, I've got her head tilted back.

CC: Is there any sign of your boyfriend [OMITTED]?

Caller: No.

CC: Okay, tell me if anything changes. Are there any dogs in the house, darling?

Caller: No. Oh, the police are here. The police are here.

CC: Are they inside the house, darling?

Caller: Aye.

CC: All right, darling.

Caller: And the ambulance man's here as well.

CC: Okay, I'll leave you with them, then.

Caller: Okay.

CC: All right, bye.

Caller: Thank you so much.

CC: That's no bother.

Caller: And thank that other guy as well.

CC: I will, darling. Bye-bye.

Caller: Bye.

If you enjoyed *Thurso*, why not try our other Armley Press titles? Available from Amazon and through UK bookshops.

Ray Brown: In All Beginnings
Mark Connors: Stickleback
Mark Connors: Tom Tit and the Maniacs
A.J. Kirby: The Lost Boys of Prometheus City
John Lake: Hot Knife
John Lake: Blowback
John Lake: Speedbomb
John Lake: Amy and the Fox
Mick McCann: Coming Out as a Bowie Fan in Leeds, Yorkshire, England
Mick McCann: Nailed
Mick McCann: How Leeds Changed the World: Encyclopaedia Leeds
Chris Nickson: Leeds, the Biography: A History of Leeds in Short Stories
Nathan O'Hagan: The World is (Not) a Cold Dead Place
Nathan O'Hagan: Out of the City
Samantha Priestley: Reliability of Rope
Samantha Priestley: A Bad Winter
David Siddall: Breaking Even
K.D. Thomas: Fogbow and Glory
Michael Yates: 20 Stories High

Visit us at www.armleypress.com and look for Armley Press on Facebook and Twitter.

CPSIA information can be obtained
at www.ICGtesting.com
Printed in the USA
BVHW070808150419
545531BV00001B/262/P